TASTE OF SURRENDER

FORBIDDEN SERIES
BOOK 4

KIMBERLY KNIGHT

RACHEL LYN ADAMS

No portion of this book may be reproduced, scanned, or distributed in any print or electronic form without permission.

This book is a work of fiction and any resemblance to any persons, living or dead, places, events or occurrences, is purely coincidental. The characters and storylines are created from the author's imagination or are used fictitiously. The subject matter is not appropriate for minors. Please note this novel contains profanity, explicit sexual situations, and alcohol consumption.

TASTE OF SURRENDER

Copyright © 2024 Kimberly Knight and Rachel Lyn Adams

Published by Kimberly Knight and Rachel Lyn Adams

Cover art © Indie Sage

Cover Image Photographer © Wander Aguiar

All rights reserved.

1

JASPER

FIVE YEARS AGO – SIXTEEN YEARS OLD

WHILE I ZONED OUT LISTENING TO MR. WILSON DRONE ON ABOUT THE Industrial Revolution, I felt my phone vibrate in my pocket. I waited until he looked down at his laptop before grabbing my cell to check my messages.

> Jeremy: Meet me in the locker room at lunch

It took a lot of effort to hold back the laughter bubbling up when the text from the guy who I'd been messing around with was quickly followed by several eggplant emojis.

A couple months ago, during our sophomore year spring break, we began *hanging out* on the down-low. We weren't officially dating, and there was no chance of us ever becoming a couple. He was firmly in the closet with zero plans to come out anytime soon, and I wasn't interested in anything serious. Our situationship was mainly based on teenage hormones and convenience. The fact he was hot didn't hurt either.

> **Me:** Won't it be locked?

> **Jeremy:** Don't worry. I took care of it

As soon as the bell rang, I packed up and headed in the opposite direction of the cafeteria and made my way to meet him.

Glancing around, I made sure no one was nearby before opening the door, which was propped open with a folded piece of paper, and entered the locker room. It was completely silent as I walked toward the back where the showers were located. When I reached the last stall, an arm reached out from behind the curtain and pulled me inside.

"What the—" I yelped, and then Jeremy attacked my mouth with his.

As we pulled apart, I noticed he was wearing nothing but boxers that did little to cover the wood he was sporting. "Why are you practically naked?" I chuckled.

He shrugged. "Figured I'd save us a little time."

Up until now, we'd only made out with a few hand jobs thrown in, so I wasn't sure why he felt it was necessary to strip down to his underwear.

"If you think I'm going to jerk you off at school, I'm afraid you're going to be disappointed."

"Why?" He stepped closer, caging me in against the tile wall. "No one's here except us."

"Yeah, where's Coach Baker?"

"He left for lunch and didn't notice me prop the door open. So, we're all alone."

Almost on cue, I heard someone call out, "Jeremy, you in here?"

We could hear several sets of footsteps heading in our direction. I looked at Jeremy, whose face had turned pale.

"Fuck, fuck, fuck," he muttered.

After a few seconds, it sounded as though the group was leaving, and Jeremy sagged against the wall opposite me, letting out a breath.

Just as I thought we were in the clear, the curtain was yanked back, and Dustin, Jeremy's best friend and teammate, stared at us, his mouth open in surprise.

"What the fuck is going on here?" he asked.

Jeremy's gaze flicked between me and his friend before he grabbed his clothes from the bench outside the stall and started getting dressed. "I don't know, man. I had grabbed a shower after PE, and then Jasper came in here and tried to kiss me."

My eyes widened at his lame attempt to lie. How stupid did these guys have to be to believe I randomly decided to approach someone in the shower and proposition him while I was still fully-clothed? Besides, it was obvious Jeremy hadn't showered since everything was dry.

"Guys, get a load of this," Dustin yelled, and the group he'd come in with gathered around us, all of them laughing at the sight in front of them. "Fairy boy over here tried to make a move on Jeremy."

Clearly, they were pretty fucking stupid.

I rolled my eyes. "That's not what happened."

"Dude, no one wants your gay ass hitting on them," Dustin continued despite what I said.

"Yeah," Jeremy added while buttoning his pants. "I definitely didn't want that."

I glared at the guy I now saw for the asshole he was. I had been willing to keep his secret, but he had no problem throwing me under the bus to save himself. I threw my hands in the air. "I'm outta here."

I shoved past Dustin so I could leave, but he grabbed my arm before I got too far and said, "Don't let me catch you looking at any of us in here when we have gym together. I won't be as understanding as Jeremy."

I pulled away from Dustin's grip and saw my older brother Jesse storming toward us. "What the fuck is going on here?"

In the middle of everything, it took a minute to realize my brother's best friend Malachi was with him. As if the situation couldn't be more embarrassing, the guy I had a secret crush on was getting a front row seat to my mortification.

"Nothing's going on, Jesse. It's just a simple misunderstanding." I pushed on my brother's chest so we could leave before his overprotective side made matters worse. "Let's go."

For a moment, I didn't think he would budge, but after one last scowl in Dustin's direction, my brother and I began moving toward the exit.

"That's right, Jesse," Dustin spat. "Get your brother out of here. No one wants that fa—"

In a flash, Jesse grabbed him by the collar and pinned him against the wall. "The fuck did you just say?"

"N-n-nothing," Dustin choked out.

"No one talks shit about my brother. Do you understand me?" Jesse growled.

Dustin nodded, and Jesse glared at the others standing around until they all mumbled their agreement.

"Now get the hell out of here." My brother shoved Dustin away.

Everyone, including Jeremy, scrambled to the exit.

When the door slammed shut behind them, Jesse turned to me. "You okay?"

I nodded. "Yeah, but I was fine before you got here too."

"It didn't look that way to me when we came in here," Malachi cut in, and I could feel my face burn with embarrassment.

"What was going on, anyway? Did it have something to do with Jeremy and the two of you sneaking around lately?" my brother asked.

"What are you talking about?"

"Don't play dumb," he chuckled. "I've seen the two of you hanging out recently, and you guys were never friends before. It wasn't hard to put two and two together."

I glanced toward Malachi, his dark green eyes watching me closely. It wasn't a secret I was gay, and none of my brother's friends ever acted as though they had an issue with it. However, I'd dealt with my fair share of teasing and mild bullying from classmates since coming out right before my freshman year, so I never really talked about it around others.

Turning my focus back to my brother, I said, "You can't say anything. I promised him I wouldn't tell anybody."

"Even after he stood there and didn't make any effort to defend you?"

I shrugged. "Yeah. I'm not going to sink to his level."

"You're too nice of a guy," Malachi said.

I didn't know if he meant it as a compliment, but I chose to take it as one.

"Going forward, I'm going to need to approve of the guys you decide to date," Jesse interjected.

I stifled the laugh trying to escape. "Are you kidding me?"

"No." Jesse crossed his arms over his chest. "You deserve better than some asshole letting you get bullied and not having the balls to stand up for you."

My brother may have only been two years older than me, but ever since he'd caught a couple of kids giving me a hard time after I came out, he sometimes acted more like he was my dad.

"Knowing my luck, you'll find a problem with every guy I try to date," I muttered.

"You're probably right. But at least I can make sure no one messes with my baby brother."

THE REST OF THE SCHOOL DAY PASSED WITHOUT ANY MORE ISSUES. After my last period, I went to the library to work on an English essay before finally heading home.

Walking down the street toward my house, I heard my brother's band practicing in our garage. Sometimes, I would listen to them play, but since I'd stayed late at school, I wanted to get inside and help my mom make dinner. Cooking was something I enjoyed, and over the years, I found myself spending more and more time in the kitchen.

With a quick wave to the guys as I passed, I made my way into the house. After dropping off my backpack in my room, I went to the kitchen, where Mom was chopping tomatoes.

"What are we having for dinner?" I asked as I washed my hands.

"It's Tuesday, so tacos, of course."

I chuckled. "Sounds good to me."

While she finished with the tomatoes, I grabbed a couple of avocados. I always made my guac on Taco Tuesday.

"Before I forget, I saw your EpiPen on your dresser while putting some clean clothes in your room. You need to remember to keep that with you."

"Sorry about that," I replied. The summer before, I'd been stung by a bee for the first time and ended up with a severe reaction and was rushed to the ER. Ever since then, my parents had been nervous about it happening again. "I'll make sure I have one in my backpack, and I'll leave the other one here."

"Good. Now, how was school today?"

"It was fine except when Jesse decided to play *super brother*," I chuckled.

"What do you mean?"

I didn't want to get into all the specifics, but maybe she'd tell Jesse to chill a little bit. "It wasn't a big deal. Me and this other guy had a misunderstanding, and Jesse thought he needed to swoop in to protect me."

"He just has your best interest at heart."

"I know, Mom."

I understood, but sometimes I wished Jesse realized I needed to work things out on my own. Maybe with him graduating in a couple of weeks, he'd start to let go a little bit.

A moment later the door leading to the garage opened, and Malachi entered the kitchen. My gaze lingered on his abs as he lifted his T-shirt to wipe the sweat off his forehead. Even though he and my brother were musicians, they often worked out together, and he was sporting a six-pack I fantasized running my hands over.

Shaking my head to rid my mind of things I had no business

thinking of with my mom standing next to me—and because he was my brother's best friend—

I quickly averted my eyes but not before Malachi gave me a knowing smirk.

Fuck my life.

"Are you done practicing?" Mom asked him.

"Not yet. We're just taking a quick break and I came in for some water, if that's okay."

"Of course. Help yourself."

"Thanks, Mrs. B." He flashed her a smile before opening the fridge and pulling out a couple of bottles.

"Want to stay for dinner?" Mom offered, always willing to feed our friends. "We're having tacos."

He looked at me. "Are you making your guac?"

My cheeks flushed as they often did anytime Malachi talked to me. "Yep."

"Then count me in." He started to leave, but shot me a wink just before he walked through the door.

Did Malachi Danvers just flirt with me?

2

MALACHI

One Year Later – Nineteen Years Old

Every year at the end of the summer before school started up again, my family and Jesse's would go camping at a lake an hour or so from where we lived. We'd fish, rent kayaks, hike, and also play games like disc golf, horseshoes, volleyball and cornhole. It was a blast, so even though Jesse and I had graduated last year, we still went with our folks.

And Jasper.

Jasper Bennett, my best friend's younger brother.

The summer before he started high school, he told all of us he was gay. I'd always thought he was cute, but, I knew he was off limits because if things were to happen between me and him, Jesse would cut off my balls.

Besides, no one knew I was bi. Not even my best friends. Before graduating, I was known around school as a ladies' man.

And I was.

Every chick wanted a piece of me, especially when they heard me sing. Who was I to deny them? I could melt their panties off as I serenaded them. It was kinda my thing and that hadn't changed since leaving high school.

What had changed in the last year was I'd finally hooked up with a guy.

One night, I went to a gay nightclub that had an eighteen and over night. I was nervous and excited as I walked into Chrome alone, and I was instantly drawn to a guy sitting at the bar. We hit it off and ended up fooling around in his car. We hadn't had sex, but having his rough hands work me as he blew me had been a whole new experience, one that'd made me come harder than I ever had with a girl.

With X Ambassadors blaring through the speakers of my yellow Jeep Wrangler Sport, I took the exit for the lake as I followed behind my parents. I'd opted to drive so we could bring more stuff for the week, and Jesse rode with me. His folks, Jasper and Jasper's friend were already at the campsite. I was looking forward to seeing Jasper shirtless for seven days.

Jesse turned down the stereo and said, "I was thinking we should apply to be on *The Band Showdown*."

I furrowed my brow as I glanced at him. "The reality show?"

"Yeah, bro. How else are we going to catch a break?"

Our band, Surrender, had been playing together for six years. It was me, Jesse and our best friends, Elliott and Silas. Jesse was our lead guitarist and backup vocals, Silas was the drummer, Elliott played bass, and I was the lead singer and played a few chords here and there when I needed to. Our sound had a pop-rock feel, and we covered bands like X Ambassadors, Twenty One Pilots, and Imagine Dragons. We had a few songs we'd written ourselves, but mostly, we played what people knew.

"I don't know." I blew out a breath. "Maybe we'll get lucky and someone will discover us when we're playing at Flanagan's."

"Right." Jesse snorted. "I think we'll have a better chance trying out for a reality show than praying someone will stumble upon us at some random Irish pub."

"Have you mentioned this to Elliott and Silas?"

"Nah." He shook his head. "Just thought of it right now."

"Well, I guess we can ask them when we're back home."

"I'll look into all the details tonight."

"All right." I nodded and pulled into the parking lot at the campground. After parking beside my parents, we piled out, including my sister, Norah, and her friend Gabby from my parent's car. We all got to work unloading our vehicles and then walked to the campsite where Jasper and his parents were setting up one of the tents. I saw no sign of Jasper's friend around. *Interesting.*

After we said our hellos, we started to set up our tents too. The entire time, I couldn't help but steal glimpses of Jasper—his dirty blond hair reflecting the sunlight, the faint sheen of sweat glistening on his tanned skin. He flashed me a smile when he caught me looking once, and my heart did a little flip, despite the familiar warning bells ringing in my head.

"No friend?" I asked him.

"AJ couldn't make it."

"Ah."

While hammering stakes into the ground and securing the guy lines, I glanced over my shoulder and caught Jasper looking at me. And because I couldn't help myself, I winked at him.

"So, what's the plan for tonight?" Jesse asked as we got the final stake in the ground.

I shrugged. "Probably the usual. You know, a bonfire, roast some marshmallows, scare the shit out of Norah and her friend with ghost stories."

Jesse grinned. "Yeah, probably, but maybe a little night fishing? That was fun last year."

I nodded. "Yeah, it was."

As we finished setting up camp, I looked around at the other campsites, wondering if I might find a girl to take my mind off of the guy I couldn't have.

Mom and Mrs. Bennett set out chips and drinks for all of us while Jasper and Mr. Bennett manned the grill, cooking burgers and hot dogs for everyone. After we all had our plates, we gathered around the crackling fire and pigged out.

Once our parents went to bed, Jesse and I grabbed our poles and headed toward the shore to fish, but neither one of us caught a bite.

THE NEXT MORNING, I ROLLED OVER TO SEE JASPER WASN'T IN HIS sleeping bag. I climbed out of mine, and left Jesse to continue sleeping in the tent.

"Morning," I greeted my friend's brother as he stood next to one of the coolers.

"Morning," he replied and cracked open an energy drink. After Jesse and I had fished—or tried to—we'd come back to the camp and found our parents asleep and Jasper playing cards with Norah and Gabby. I had no idea if he went to bed or not.

I grabbed a fruit punch energy drink and opened it. "How are you even awake right now?"

"Who said I went to sleep?" He smirked.

I stepped closer and lowered my voice. "If I didn't know better, I'd think you stayed out late to hook up with Gabby."

He snorted a laugh. "Nothing like that. I don't think it was much longer after you and Jesse went to bed."

"Guess I passed out. Didn't even hear you come in."

"Or I'm just good at sneaking around."

A grin spread across my face. "Good to know."

Before he could reply, the zipper of my parents' tent opened and both of them crawled out.

"Morning," I greeted.

"You boys are up early," Mom stated as she stretched.

Dad went straight for the instant coffee supply. "After hearing you kids playing cards all night, I expected all of you to sleep until noon."

Jasper shook his head. "Needed to get breakfast started for everyone and then I was thinking of going for a hike before it gets too hot."

"That sounds like a good plan." Mom grabbed a coffee cup.

"That does," I said. "Maybe I'll go too."

"Go where?" Jesse yawned behind me.

I turned as Jasper replied, "For a hike."

"Maybe you should bring your sister and Gabby," Mom suggested. "Gabby's never been here, remember?"

When I said maybe I'd go too, I didn't mean as a group. "Yeah, sure, whatever." Jasper cocked an eyebrow, and I shrugged slightly. "Hope you didn't want to go alone."

"Nah." He shook his head. "The more the merrier."

AFTER BREAKFAST, WE *KIDS* CHANGED INTO CLOTHES TO GO HIKING. As I waited for everyone else, Gabby walked out of the tent she was sharing with Norah and sat next to me on the picnic table.

"How far are we going to hike?" she asked.

I lifted a shoulder. "I don't know."

"What if we see a snake?"

"Then we see a snake."

"What if we see a bear?"

"Then we see a bear."

She ran her finger down my bicep. "Will you protect me from a bear?"

I shifted uncomfortably. "You're Norah's friend. I don't think she'd be too happy if I let anything happen to you."

Gabby leaned in a little closer. "Oh, come on. Just because I'm friends with your sister doesn't mean we can't have a little fun."

I stood up, glancing around to see if anyone was coming. "I think we should focus on the hike. Besides, I'm sure there won't be any bears."

"You're no fun," she teased with a little pout on her lips.

I rubbed the back of my neck, trying to find the right words to put a stop to her attempt at flirting, but before I could, Jasper came out of the tent, saving me. For a split second, I could have sworn I saw a look of jealousy cross over his face.

Once everyone was ready, we headed out, but not even five minutes into the walk through the woods, Gabby stopped and whined, "Can we go back now?"

All of us turned, and Norah asked, "You want to go back already?"

"Yeah. I'm not much of an outdoorsy person," Gabby replied.

"You came camping," I deadpanned.

Gabby lifted a shoulder. "I thought we'd swim in the lake the whole time."

"We're doing that after," Jesse stated.

"It's fine. Let's go back." Norah blew out a breath and gave me a tight smile. I returned it and the girls turned and walked back toward the campsite.

"Chicks, man. Am I right?" Jesse clapped me on the back.

"You know it." I chuckled and then glanced at Jasper. He rolled his eyes, and we started back on the trail.

As we hiked along the path, the sun filtered through the trees, providing a little bit of shade from the heat at times. Jesse led the way, and I couldn't help but notice Jasper lagging.

"Hey, you doing okay?" I asked, dropping back to walk alongside him.

He shrugged. "Just tired, I guess."

"Yeah, only a few hours of sleep will do that to you."

"Thought the energy drink would help."

"Only temporarily."

"Right." He snorted.

A few more steps down the trail, a buzzing caught my attention, and then suddenly, Jasper yelped. "Ow! What the ..."

As I looked over at him, panic surged through me as I remembered his allergy. "Shit! Were you just stung by a bee?"

He nodded, his bright blue eyes wide. "Yeah, and I don't have my EpiPen on me. It's back at camp in my bag."

Without hesitation, Jesse bolted back down the trail as he called out, "I'll go get it!"

I knelt beside Jasper as he sank to the ground, his head between his legs as if his lungs were closing up. I supposed they were, and my heart thumped rapidly as I tried not to show how worried I was about him. "Hey," I murmured, "you're gonna be okay. Jesse will get your EpiPen, and everything will be fine."

Jasper managed a weak smile as he lifted his head slightly. "You're right, it's just ... scary, you know?"

"Yeah," I admitted, my heart aching for him. "But you're not alone. I'm right here with you."

As I spoke, I felt something wash over me. It was like a warmth spreading through my chest that had nothing to do with the summer sun. At that moment, with Jasper's hand in mine, I realized just how deeply I cared for him. I could tell myself it was only a crush, but deep down, I knew it was more.

"Malachi," Jasper whispered. "Thank you."

I met his gaze. "For what?"

"For being here," he said simply, his eyes searching mine.

"Always." I couldn't take the silence as we waited, so I finally asked, "Wanna play a game?"

"Sure, what game?"

"How about the questions game?" I suggested.

He nodded. "All right. You ask first."

"Okay." I thought for a moment. "If you could visit any place in the world, where would you go?"

"Hmmm well, I've always wanted to see the Northern Lights. I think it would be so cool to see."

"Yeah, it would," I agreed, glad to see a spark of enthusiasm in his eyes. "Your turn."

He hesitated for a beat, then asked, "If you could have any superpower, what would it be?"

I didn't have to think twice. "Definitely flying. Imagine soaring above the trees, feeling the wind in your hair, and getting to places faster."

Jasper nodded. "Yeah, that would be awesome."

We continued exchanging questions, each one a brief distraction from the worry gnawing inside me. I could see rashes start to appear on his arm, but I didn't say anything because I didn't want to draw attention to it. He was already having difficulty breathing with each passing minute, and that gave us both enough to panic about.

Finally, Jesse ran up the trail and I stood, moving out of the way so he could get to Jasper. In a flash, he stuck his brother in the leg and administered the medication, and I felt my body relax.

Jesse handed Jasper a bottle of water. "You good?"

"I will be. Thank you." Jasper took a sip. "Mom and Dad freaking out?"

Jesse shook his head. "They weren't there."

"Thank god."

"Well, I'm just happy I didn't need to give you mouth-to-mouth." I winked at Jasper.

He chuckled. "I wouldn't have pushed you away."

"Okay, gross." Jesse shuddered playfully.

"Are you ready to head back to camp? We can take it slow," I said to Jasper.

"Give me a few minutes."

Once he was ready, I walked next to him, then said low so only he could hear me, "I wouldn't push you away if you kissed me, either."

AFTER EVERYONE CALLED IT A NIGHT, JESSE, JASPER, AND I CRAWLED into our tent. Each of us found entertainment on our phones as I lay in the middle of them. The afternoon had taken a turn because once we were back at the campsite, Jasper had gone with his parents to the hospital to get checked out. Luckily, it wasn't far and they weren't away but for a few hours. Once they had come back and said everything was going to be okay, I had felt a weight lift from me.

"So, we have to submit a video," Jesse said out of the blue.

I turned my head to face him. "For what?"

"For *The Band Showdown*," he replied.

"You guys are trying out for a reality show?" Jasper asked.

"Your brother wants to," I answered.

"It can't hurt," Jesse said.

He was right, but it had never crossed my mind until he had suggested it the day before. Maybe it would be our big break.

I glanced at Jasper. "Will you vote for us?"

"No way! I've heard you guys play." He grinned.

A smile tugged at my lips as I knew he was joking. "Ouch. You know we're the best band around."

"I'm teasing. Yes, I'll vote for you guys."

"I'm still doing research," Jesse advised, not batting an eye at what me and Jasper were joking about. "But yeah, we totally should do this."

After some time, Jesse shut off his phone and curled on his side, turning away from us. Once I thought he was asleep, I rolled onto my side and faced Jasper. Reaching out tentatively, my fingers brushed against his hand where it rested between us. He met my gaze and furrowed his brow.

"Are you still doing okay after what happened earlier?" I whispered.

He nodded, his lips curling into a faint smile. "Yeah."

"Good. Have to admit, I was pretty freaked out."

"You were?" He rolled so we were face to face.

"Hell yeah. You mean a lot to me."

His eyes widened. "I do?"

"Why is that so hard to believe?"

He shrugged the best he could while lying on his side. "I don't know. You're my brother's best friend."

"What if I wanted to be more?"

He stared at me for a few long seconds. "More?"

I nodded. "Yeah."

"Are you serious?"

Leaning forward, I closed the distance between us, my lips meeting his in a gentle, light press. Jasper's hand moved to cup my cheek and deepened the kiss. It was like nothing I had ever experienced before, and the electricity between us sent shivers down my spine.

Once we pulled apart, I asked, "Does that answer your question?"

"That one, but I have a lot more."

3

JASPER

B̲ETWEEN WHAT HAPPENED ON OUR HIKE THE DAY BEFORE AND IN THE tent last night, I once again got very little sleep.

Never did I think I would get the chance to kiss Malachi Danvers because until yesterday, I thought he was as straight as they come.

Yet, he kissed me.

Or maybe I kissed him.

It didn't really matter who leaned in first. All I knew was it had been amazing.

As the morning light drifted into our tent, I lay in my sleeping bag, replaying everything in my head. I remembered him saying how he wanted more. Unfortunately, my brother mumbled something in his sleep, putting an end to our conversation before I could ask Malachi what he'd meant.

While he and Jesse continued to sleep, I decided to get up and start making breakfast. Cooking always helped clear my head whenever I was stressed about school or something else like a crush on my brother's best friend. It was also good practice for the job I was starting in a few weeks at a local diner.

Digging through the coolers, I grabbed the ingredients I needed to make French toast and scrambled eggs. I'd helped plan out the menu for the week and picked this specific meal because I knew it was Malachi's favorite.

I was so wrapped up in getting the food ready, I didn't realize anyone else was awake until the guy I couldn't stop thinking about started to speak.

"Something looks good." He stepped close behind me, and I could feel his body heat wash over me, which sent a shiver down my spine.

"I know you like French toast."

"I wasn't talking about—"

"Is breakfast ready yet?" Jesse called out as he exited the tent. "I'm starving."

Malachi took a step back as I grumbled, "Not yet."

"We going fishing again today?" my brother asked his friend as he spooned some instant coffee into a mug.

"Sure," Malachi replied, and then turned toward me. "Do you want to come with us?"

"You know Jasper hates fishing," Jesse interjected before I could answer.

He wasn't wrong, but it was nice for Malachi to want to include me, especially since my friend AJ had to back out of coming with us at the last minute. "Yeah. Sitting around, messing with worms all day isn't really my idea of a good time, but I'll be ready to cook whatever you guys catch."

A little while later, everyone else joined us at the picnic table for breakfast. Gabby took a seat next to Malachi, which wasn't surprising. When we'd played cards, she wouldn't stop talking about how cute he was. While I wasn't happy to hear about her crush, Norah had been annoyed and pleaded with her to not talk about her brother like that. It made me wonder if Jesse would have the same reaction if he knew what Malachi and I had been up to the night before. Who was I kidding? Jesse would be more than annoyed at his best friend. And maybe me.

"Jasper, I gotta say, your cooking gets better and better every time you make something," Mr. Danvers said around a bit of French toast, taking my attention away from Gabby and Malachi.

I swallowed a forkful of eggs and smiled. "Thank you."

"Yeah, this is way better than Mom's." Norah chuckled.

"Gee, thanks." Mrs. Danvers glared playfully at her daughter. "But I don't disagree. Have you thought about becoming a chef one day?"

I shrugged. "I just got a job as a prep cook, but I don't know if I'm good enough to run my own kitchen."

Everyone quickly disagreed with my statement, and I could feel my cheeks heat at their compliments. I wasn't one who liked to be the center of attention, and their praise was a little overwhelming.

"So, what's everyone's plans today?" Malachi asked the others. "Jesse and I are going fishing."

As everybody began chatting about what they wanted to do, I looked at Malachi. He gave me a sly grin, and I wondered if he'd changed the subject because he could tell I'd been uncomfortable.

I had always assumed he never noticed me, and if he did, he only saw me as Jesse's little brother. But maybe he'd been looking at me the same way as I had him all these years.

Malachi and I didn't get a second alone for the remainder of the week. We shared occasional glances, and there were times I swore he purposely brushed against me, but I never had the opportunity to ask him why he'd kissed me or any of the other questions I had.

That changed as we broke down camp, and my brother's phone rang.

"You guys got this?" Jesse asked. "I've been waiting for Liv to call."

Olivia was his girlfriend of three years, and she usually went camping with us but she was spending this summer in Europe with her family.

"Yeah. We're good," Malachi said, pulling out one of the tent stakes.

Jesse walked toward the trees, and I moved over to the side where Malachi was working out of sight of everyone else. The second I stepped beside him, he flashed me his megawatt smile. The same one that had girls swooning at their gigs.

"Did you have fun this week?" he asked.

"It's definitely been interesting."

He stopped what he was doing and faced me. "Interesting. How?"

"Are you really going to make me say it?"

He shrugged, the smile never leaving his face. "Yes."

"Fine." I chuckled. "I found it interesting that all this time, I thought you were into girls, yet you kissed me."

"Well, I am into girls."

My gaze dropped to my feet. "Oh."

"But I also happen to be bi, so I'm not *only* into girls."

"Oh," I repeated. "I didn't know that."

"No one does," he admitted.

"Why not tell my brother? He didn't have a problem when I came out, and I know he wouldn't have an issue with you either."

"You're probably right." He let out a breath. "It's just ... I've got this image as a ladies' man I created with the band, and I'm not sure if telling the guys would change things and cause problems."

"I guess that makes sense." No way was I going to judge someone else's journey. When and how they chose to share intimate details about their life with others was their business.

"Regardless of whether or not people know, I meant it when I said I wanted more the other night." He stuffed the stakes into the tent bag.

"You did?"

He nodded. "Yeah. But Jesse would kill me if he knew I was messing around with his little brother."

My shoulders slumped. "I get it."

"Hey." He lifted my chin with his finger. "That doesn't mean I—"

Before he could say anything more, Jesse came back. "What's taking you guys so long? Everyone else is ready to go."

"Well, if someone had stayed to help us instead of bailing to talk to his girlfriend, then we'd be done already," Malachi scolded playfully.

"Don't be mad you can only get a chick for one night," my brother teased.

Malachi's eyes cut to me briefly before he responded, "Nah, man. I'm not looking to get tied down and practically married at nineteen like you."

"Don't hate. You know you love Liv too."

"Yeah, she's not bad." Malachi grinned.

After we finished putting the tent away, I drove away with my parents. I stared out the window thinking about our kiss and wondering if it would happen again.

Several weeks had passed since we returned from the lake. Between school and my new job, I hadn't seen Malachi, and I was beginning to wonder if he was avoiding me.

I'd just started making dinner when I heard the front door open and close. Soon Jesse rounded the corner, and when he saw me standing at the stove, he asked, "What are you making?"

I stirred the onions I was sautéing. "Salisbury steak, mashed potatoes, and a salad."

"Nice." He grabbed a bottle of water from the fridge and chugged half of it. "Can you make enough for Malachi too? We're going to hang out over here and watch some movies tonight."

"Uh sure," I replied, wondering if things were going to be awkward.

Whenever they had one of their movie nights, Malachi usually ended up staying over, and I was both excited and nervous to have him around.

"Cool. I'm going to take a shower and get the gym smell off of me."

"Good, because you reek."

"You're just jealous because you don't have arms like this." My brother flexed his biceps and gave me a cheesy grin.

"Hopefully, you've been working out your neck so it can hold up that gigantic head of yours," I teased as he started toward his room.

A few minutes later, the doorbell rang, and since my parents weren't home from work quite yet, I had no choice but to answer it.

"Oh ... hey," Malachi greeted me as I pulled the door open.

"Hey," I replied and stepped aside so he could come in. "Haven't seen you for a while." I closed the door behind him and headed back to the kitchen.

He followed me. "Yeah. I've been busy."

"Really? Because if I didn't know any better, I'd say you've been avoiding me."

He let out a breath. "Look, I probably gave you mixed signals with us kissing and then not talking to you. I promise that wasn't my intention."

"You don't have to explain yourself," I said, mostly because I wasn't sure how I would handle it if he told me he regretted what he'd said while we were camping.

"But—"

I turned on the burner under the pot of potatoes so they could come to a boil. "It's okay. I promise."

"No, it's not." He spun me around. "I wasn't lying when I said I wanted more, and I haven't been able to stop thinking about kissing you again."

"Malachi ..." I whispered.

He wasn't the only one who couldn't stop thinking about it, and I desperately wanted us to do it again. Thankfully, I didn't have to wait long. He took a step forward and leaned down, fusing our mouths together. His hands wrapped around my neck, and he pulled me closer. Needing more, I parted my lips so he could deepen the kiss. Our tongues swirled together, and I could taste a hint of mint on his breath.

I could have kissed him for hours, but our moment was cut short by pounding footsteps as my brother came down the hallway. Immediately, I pushed away from Malachi and turned my focus back to cooking dinner.

From the corner of my eye, I watched as they pounded fists and started talking about the reality show their band had submitted an audition tape for.

A short time later, my parents arrived. While the five of us sat down for dinner together, it took everything in my power not to stare at Malachi from across the table. I hoped we'd get another minute alone tonight.

AFTER MY PARENTS WENT TO BED, JESSE STARTED LOOKING FOR A movie to watch. "What are you in the mood for?" he asked Malachi.

"I don't know." He shrugged. "Anything in particular you want to watch, Jasper?"

I looked up from the game I'd been playing on my phone, surprised he'd asked me.

"Who said he can hang out with us?" Jesse huffed, but I could tell he was teasing. "I guess if he makes us popcorn, he can watch the movie too."

"Fine. I'll make some, but you better pick something good." I glared playfully at my brother.

"I'll go grab some drinks," Malachi offered and followed me to the kitchen.

The second my brother couldn't see us anymore, Malachi pushed me against the wall and we became a tangle of arms, lips, and tongues. It was only our third kiss, but I was quickly becoming addicted to the taste of him.

When we pulled away to catch our breath, he pressed his forehead against mine. "The only thing I thought about during dinner was kissing you again. Even though it's probably not a good idea, I just can't get enough of you."

"Me either. I've had a crush on you for a while," I confessed, deciding to be upfront about my feelings if we were going to continue kissing every time we were alone.

"Really?"

"Uh huh."

"I wish we didn't have to hide, but Jesse can't find out about us."

"I know," I sighed, wishing the same thing.

"But I can't stay away from you anymore."

My shift at Belle's Diner was over in thirty minutes. With my eighteenth birthday still a few weeks away, I was limited on the hours I was allowed to work and got off at around the same time as the usual Friday night rush of teens trying to grab a bite to eat before curfew. As I was about to clock out, I could hear the crowds of people filling up the restaurant.

"Jasper, I've got an order here for hash browns with cheese and jalapeños on top. Can you take care of that before you leave?" Lyle, the head cook, called out.

I knew only one person who liked his hash browns like that, and I'd been told he might stop by tonight. I peeked out through the pass to confirm my suspicions, and as I expected, Jesse was sitting at a booth with his friends. But it was the person sitting across from him who had my heart racing.

"On it," I shouted back and got to work on the potatoes.

As I finished up with Jesse's food, Lyle set out the other plates for their table.

"All right, I'm outta here," I told him and then turned to Bonnie, one of the servers. "I'll take this order out to table six."

"Thanks, hun," she replied as she filled some drinks.

Weaving my way through the crowd, I made my way to my brother's table. "Hey guys," I greeted. "So, who ordered what?"

After they all told me which meals were whose, Malachi looked up and smiled. "I didn't know you were working tonight."

He was full of shit because we had texted about me having to work and how he was going to convince the others to stop by after their show at Flanagan's where they were the opening gig. Playing along, I replied, "Yeah, I just finished, actually."

"Pull up a chair and hang with us for a few," he suggested.

"Are you sure?" I asked, glancing at my brother to make sure he was cool with me staying.

Jesse nodded. "Yeah, but I'm not sharing my hash browns."

"Be nice." Olivia shoved him playfully before pushing her plate closer to me. "You can have some of my fries."

"Thanks." I grabbed a fry and popped it into my mouth. "And don't worry, Jesse, I already tried a bite while I made them," I teased.

He rolled his eyes. "Whatever."

I chuckled. "So, how was the show tonight?"

"It totally rocked," Silas said around a forkful of waffle.

Elliott nodded. "The chicks were fucking hot too."

"Yeah, it was fun," Malachi added mildly.

Jesse snorted. "Fun? You walked out of there with a handful of phone numbers and offers to hook up. I'd say it was more than fun for you."

My body stiffened, and Malachi's hand squeezed my leg under the table. "It's not a big deal. Some of them were pretty drunk and would have talked to whoever they saw first."

"Whatever, man. They were all over you," Jesse argued.

"Anyway." Malachi chuckled, but I could tell by the slight grimace on his face when he looked at me, he wasn't happy about what Jesse said. "Are you heading straight home from here?"

"That's the plan," I replied.

"Think I can catch a ride with you? Jesse was going to drop me off before going to Olivia's, but I'm tired of playing third wheel with them. And since we're going in the same direction …"

"Yeah, I can take you home."

We all continued to chat while they finished their meals. When it was time to go, we headed to the parking lot together. Silas hopped into Elliott's pickup while Olivia and Jesse climbed inside my brother's car.

Once they drove away, Malachi followed me to my ten-year-old Honda Civic.

"I'm glad our little plan worked, and you were able to stop by tonight," I said as I pulled out of the parking lot.

"Me too. Although your brother wanted to go straight to Olivia's after our show. Thank goodness she was hungry too."

"So, she unknowingly helped us sneak around behind her boyfriend's back. Let's hope she never figures that out."

He snorted a laugh. "Yeah. I doubt she would be willing to keep something like that from Jesse."

The drive to our neighborhood only took a few minutes, and as I pulled up to his house, Malachi turned to face me. "I don't plan on calling any of the women who gave me their numbers, by the way."

"Don't worry about it. I've been to your shows before, so I know that happens a lot."

He grabbed my hand. "It does, but I also don't want you to think I'm out trying to hook up with a bunch of people. I know things are complicated for us—"

"You don't need to explain. I understand how things have to be. Although, it doesn't mean I like hearing about women throwing themselves at you."

"Well, I can promise the only person on my mind tonight was you." He grinned before leaning forward to kiss me.

His hand cupped my cheek, his thumb stroking my jaw as his tongue traced my lips, and I opened for him. Our mouths moved together as he pulled me closer, and for a few moments, everything else seemed to disappear. There was no overprotective brother or need to hide. It was just Malachi and me giving in to the feelings we could no longer deny.

4

MALACHI

After taking a swig of my fruit punch energy drink, I set the can down on the beat-up wooden coffee table in Jesse's garage where the guys and I practiced for gigs and just to play. "Let's kick things off with 'Sober'," I said and moved to my microphone.

Jesse's fingers danced across the strings of his Epiphone Les Paul, Elliott joined in with his Fender, Silas beat his sticks against his set, and I belted out the lyrics to the song by Bad Wolves. I lost myself in the words, closing my eyes as I sang about alcohol addiction from the loved one's side.

Even though the guys and I dreamed of becoming rock stars, I wasn't sure if I was down to party non-stop with drugs and alcohol like rock stars were known for. My dad's father struggled with alcohol addiction and after seeing him lose his family by getting divorced and his kids not wanting contact with him and then losing his job because he was always drunk, I didn't want that for my future. Sure, Jesse and I snuck a few beers at his parents' when I'd stayed the night, but it didn't compare to the fifth of vodka my grandfather drank each night. I didn't want to be blackout drunk and not remember any point in time. I wanted to remember it all, especially if we became famous.

Still with my eyes closed, I sang the words as I pictured myself up on a stage in an arena filled to capacity. How the lights would shine down on us, and our fans would sing along to the songs we'd written.

As we finished the song, I opened my eyes only to meet those of Jasper's. I hadn't heard him walk up the driveway, but as our gazes collided, we both smiled.

"That sounded fantastic," he praised. "Is that the one you guys are recording for *The Band Showdown*?"

"Yeah," Jesse replied as he set his guitar on its stand. "And I think we're ready for our virtual audition."

To try-out for the show, we had to create an account on their website and select a time to do a virtual audition. Then once we recorded a three-minute song during our selected time slot, we would be emailed the results. Well, Jesse would be, because he was handling all that stuff for us.

If the casting directors liked what they heard, we would have an interview and need to submit more songs, and *then* attend the live auditions in Los Angeles. It was a long process, but like Jesse said, it was our best shot at being recognized.

"I fucking hope so," Silas stated. "I want to go to Cali and see all the half-naked chicks on the beach."

I grinned at Silas's remark, shaking my head. "Man, you and your priorities," I teased, but deep down, I couldn't help but share a bit of his excitement. Making it to the sunny shores of California was all part of the dream to hit it big.

Jasper leaned against the doorframe, a smile still on his face. "Well, when you become famous rock stars, don't forget about us little people." He chuckled.

"Never," I replied.

Jesse walked over to the table and snatched his keys. "All right guys. I gotta take the birthday boy for his first tattoo. Be here tomorrow early so we can get some more practice in before our audition."

"Cool. I gotta meet up with Donnie anyway," Silas said as he stood from his drum set.

We had all gone to high school with Donnie Pierce. He'd been a known drug dealer when we were in school and still sold Silas weed. I didn't like the dude. He thought he was badass all because he did illegal shit.

"Yeah, and I promised my mom I'd go grocery shopping with her," Elliott advised.

Silas and Elliott gave us fist bumps, then headed to their cars to drive away. I hung back, which wasn't unusual given my house was only a few doors down.

"So, getting a tattoo?" I asked Jasper and went to the table to finish my energy drink.

"Jesse talked me into it," he stated.

I met Jesse's gaze and arched a brow.

"He wanted to be lame and not do anything for his eighteenth birthday," Jesse clarified.

"No." Jasper pushed off the doorjamb. "I said I wanted to go out to dinner with my friends."

"Which you did last night. Now it's time for my present." Jesse clapped his brother on the back.

"Mind if I tag along?" I asked.

Jasper's eyes widened. "You want to come with us?"

I showed him the snake wrapping around my left arm. When I'd gotten the tattoo, I thought it was badass looking but then talking with the artist, he said in Chinese culture they were associated with luck and good fortune and that seemed fitting at the time. "Sure. I'm no stranger to ink."

"Well, let's go. Appointment is in thirty." Jesse headed to his car.

Jasper got into the back while I rode shotgun. A few miles down the road, I turned and asked Jasper, "What are you thinking about getting?"

"I don't know. My brother"—he glared at Jesse—"only told me about the appointment this morning when I opened his card."

"You mentioned you wanted a tattoo last night and I called in a favor with my guy. You should be thanking me," Jesse chimed in.

"Yeah, but I haven't thought of what to get yet," Jasper continued to protest.

"Just get something small," I suggested.

"Small?" Jesse gasped. "He's a man now. He needs something bold."

I rolled my eyes. "Don't listen to him. Just pick something you like."

Once we pulled up to the tattoo parlor, we all piled out and walked inside. The tattoo guns buzzed as we approached the front desk. When I looked over at Jasper, he was pale and beads of sweat dotted his forehead.

"Hey." I grabbed his forearm. "You don't have to do this."

He swallowed and looked up slightly at me. "It's fine. I'll get something small like you said."

"Do you want to look at some examples?" the male artist asked.

"Sure," Jasper replied.

"Just let me know what you decide." The artist placed an album in front of us and Jasper flipped the pages as the guy walked away to set up his station.

"What if Jesse and I get tattoos too?" I offered. I wasn't sure if the tattoo guy could fit us in, but I had to try to put Jasper at ease somehow.

"What would you get?" Jasper asked.

I flipped through a few pages of the book and then pointed at a set. "Well, one of us can get a sun, one a moon, and the other a star."

"I'm not getting a matching tattoo with my brother," Jesse stated, and his cell rang. He pulled it out. "It's Liv. Pick whatever. I'm paying, but I'm not getting one."

He walked out of the building, and Jasper and I returned to the album.

"Fine. What if you get a sun and I get a moon?" I offered.

"You want to get something that goes together?"

"Sure. It can be our little secret." I winked.

I watched his Adam's apple slide up and down as he swallowed. "Okay."

"Or we can both get matching crescent moons."

"I'd like that." Jasper smiled.

I grinned back. "Me too. I'll even go first if you want."

"Okay."

I wanted to lean over and kiss him, but I refrained. Instead, I called to the artist, "All right. We're ready." The guy walked over. "We're each going to get one if that's cool."

"If it's large, you'll need to come back," he replied.

"It's not," I clarified. "We're going to get small matching crescent moons on opposite wrists."

The guy blinked and then nodded. "Okay. Give me a few to get them drawn up."

As we waited, Jesse came back. "What did you decide?"

"A crescent moon," Jasper replied.

"Lame."

"I'm getting one too," I stated.

Jesse balked. "Really? Why? I thought you were joking about getting matching tattoos."

"I offered to go first since your ass is too consumed with pussy and to show *your* brother it'll be fine."

"But matching?" Jesse shook his head. "People are going to think you're dating if you get the same tattoo."

I glanced at Jasper with a smirk. The idea of dating him made me smile. "It's fine. It will be part of my collection."

Jasper nodded in agreement, though he still looked like he was going to pass out. "It's just a little something to mark my birthday. I'll even go first."

"Are you sure?" I asked.

"I'm a man now, right?" He rolled his eyes at his brother.

I chuckled. "Yeah, you are."

The artist returned with the sketches of the crescent moons, and Jasper and I exchanged a glance before nodding our approval. As he settled into the chair, I gave his shoulder a reassuring squeeze.

"You got this," I whispered.

"You sure about a crescent moon, Jasper?" Jesse asked. "Once it's on, it's on."

Jasper looked at me as he responded, "I'm sure. Let's do it."

The buzzing of the tattoo gun started as the artist got to work on the moon on his wrist. I watched his face closely, ready to offer distraction or comfort if needed. But to my surprise, he didn't flinch as each press of the needle marked his skin.

"You good?" I asked.

Jasper nodded. "Yep. Just feels like I'm being scratched."

"Yeah." I grinned. "Maybe your next one will be bigger."

"I'm not sure I'll get another one."

I snorted a laugh. "Sure you will. You'll get the bug."

Once the artist finished up, Jasper admired the new ink on the inside of his right wrist, a grin spreading across his face. "Thanks, man," he said, turning to me. "And thanks for helping me stay calm."

I shrugged, trying to play it cool. "No problem. Anytime."

With Jasper's tattoo done, it was my turn next. I settled into the chair, feeling a strange mix of excitement and nerves. But as the tattoo gun started up, and I felt the familiar sting of the needle against the inside of my left wrist, I knew that every time I looked at the moon, I'd think of the guy I shared stolen kisses with.

LATER THAT NIGHT, AFTER WE PIGGED OUT ON CHINESE TAKEOUT, WE sang "Happy Birthday" to the birthday boy, then ate cake. Even though I spent most of my time at their house, it was the first time I stayed for Jasper's birthday celebration. No one questioned why, since I was always welcome there and felt like part of the family.

"Oh, honey," Mrs. B said to Jasper. "Are you going to show us your new tattoo?"

Jesse snorted a laugh and Jasper's eyes met mine. I smiled at him and gave him a slight nod.

"Sure." He moved the sleeve of his long T-shirt up his arm,

exposing the tattoo that was covered with plastic wrap around his wrist. He lifted it to reveal the crescent moon.

"Malachi got the same one," Jesse continued mockingly.

"I'd offered because Jasper was a little nervous," I clarified.

"Aw, that was sweet of you." Mrs. B beamed.

"Why a crescent moon?" Mr. B asked.

Jasper's eyes widened, and I knew he didn't know what to say, so I answered with a shrug of my shoulder as though it was no big deal. "It was just something small. Figured it was best to get something that didn't take a long time to do."

"I didn't know he was such a baby," Jesse teased.

"Shut up!" Jasper glared at his brother.

"It can always be added to or covered up," I went on.

"Maybe you should have just given your brother the money instead of making him mark his body," Mrs. B said to Jesse.

"Meh. He'll live." Jesse stuck the last bite of his cake into his mouth.

After the cake, we gathered in the living room to watch an action movie Jasper had picked. He and I sat next to each other on one couch, Jesse lounged on the floor, not watching the movie as his focus stayed on his phone, and their parents were on the other sofa next to us.

Grabbing the blanket from the back of the couch, I draped it over me and then offered to share with Jasper. He nodded and moved closer, so I spread the blanket out over us. Our legs pressed together, and the blanket shielded our contact from view. Unable to follow along with the movie, I slowly slid my hand to his leg and trailed my fingers up his thigh. His breath caught, and he swallowed, but didn't take his stare away from the TV.

Inch by inch, my hand moved up his leg, and when I couldn't go any higher, I walked my fingers to the bulge in his shorts. He groaned and then cleared his throat before leaning over to grab his can of soda from the side table next to him. He took a sip, returned it, then leaned back. He glanced over at me, and I mouthed, "Relax."

With his family a few feet from us, I wasn't going to go any further than keeping my hand on the outside of his cargo pants. Instead, I caressed his dick and felt it stiffen beneath my touch. My own cock was hardening, like it wanted to break through the zipper of my jeans, and I wished the movie would end. I wasn't sure what would happen when it did, but since I had yet to kiss him all day, I knew I wanted to give him a proper birthday kiss before the night was over.

I looked over at his parents to see that his mom had fallen asleep, and his dad was playing a game on his phone. Jesse was still engrossed in his, probably texting with Olivia. If only everyone would go to sleep, then I could get what I really wanted.

Jasper leaned over and whispered, "You need to stop before we're caught."

I nodded and withdrew my hand. Without a word, I stood and went to the bathroom, where I waited a few minutes for my dick to calm down. Just as I was about to leave, a faint knock rapped on the door. I opened it to see Jasper on the other side.

"I told everyone I was going to bed," he said.

"Oh," I breathed.

"Jesse wants to go meet up with Olivia."

"Okay." I nodded. I got it. Jesse was in love and was just being a good brother. Now that the birthday boy was going to bed, he could leave.

"I'm going to sleep with the window open."

I blinked at Jasper's words as I tried to understand why he was telling me, and then it clicked. "Oh. Okay."

"Have a good night." He winked and walked to his room. Once I heard the click of the lock, I went back to the living room where Jesse was waiting.

"I'm headed to Liv's," he said when he saw me.

"Yeah, sure. I'll head home," I lied.

Jesse's dad turned off the TV and then woke his wife as I headed to the front door. Pretending to go to my house a few doors down, I walked down the sidewalk until Jesse got into his car and drove away. Turning back around, I moved toward the side gate of their house, opened it quietly, and then shut it softly behind me.

Tiptoeing to Jasper's window, I saw the light shining through the open window and I hurried over. "Psst," I called out.

He scrambled off his bed, rushed to the window, and whispered, "Did my parents go to bed?"

"Yeah."

"Good."

I hoisted myself up and into his bedroom. I'd never stepped foot inside it before—never needed to. It wasn't much different from Jesse's or mine. It had a full-size bed, plus a nightstand and dresser that matched. On the desk was a laptop and what looked like homework next to it. What differed from mine and his brother's room was the cookbooks scattered around instead of magazines like *Rolling Stone*.

Keeping my voice low, I said, "I like your room."

"Thanks so ... um ..."

"You want me to finish what I started?" I grinned, and he nodded. "Then get on your bed."

He did, and I climbed on beside him. He lay on his back as I once again trailed my hand up his thigh and then over to his bulge.

"You know, this would be easier if you weren't wearing pants."

"Okay," he breathed and then got to work, unbuttoning them and lowering his fly. "What about you?"

"You want my jeans off too?" I smirked.

"Fuck yeah," he replied.

"All right."

We both shed our pants, but I got off the bed to remove mine. Instead of immediately sliding in next to him, I also shucked my shirt and boxers, then straddled his lap fully naked. Leaning down, I kissed him, needing finally to taste him. As our tongues worked together, I rolled my hips; the pressure and friction made my bare cock harden against his, which was still hidden by his boxers. He moaned against my mouth, and I pulled back slightly.

"You know, I didn't give you a birthday present today." I kissed down the side of his neck.

"That's okay."

"It's not." I kissed his collarbone and then lifted his shirt to expose his stomach. "But I have the perfect gift in mind."

As I worked my way to his shaft, I grabbed ahold of his boxers and tugged them slightly down his legs. He was rock hard and my mouth watered at the sight of his erection.

Wrapping my fingers around the base of his rod, I held it up and swirled my tongue over his leaking tip. He bucked, his back arching, and I groaned as his saltiness hit my taste buds.

"You like that?" I asked.

"Abso—"

I didn't wait for him to finish speaking and took him into my hot mouth. His hands clasped the sides of my head, and his fingers threaded into my hair as I bobbed up and down and sucked him like the best fucking lollipop I'd ever had.

"I'm going to come."

I popped off his dick and smiled. "Then do it."

Returning to my task, I blew him fast and hard, my hand joining in to work in sync with my mouth. It didn't take long before his body tensed and he blew his load, the taste of him exploding over my tongue.

I swallowed it all down and then kissed my way up his stomach, to his throat, and then claimed his mouth again.

As our tongues played with each other, Jasper reached between us and fisted my rock-hard cock.

"My turn," he said against my lips.

"Nah. That wouldn't be fair. That was your birthday present." I nipped at his bottom lip.

"Are you sure?"

"There's always tomorrow." I winked as I met his gaze. "But you can still jerk me off."

And he did.

5

Jasper

Once Malachi left, I had a difficult time falling asleep. All I could do was think about his mouth wrapped around my dick. My experience was limited to a few hand jobs, so I had never been on the receiving end of a blow job or given one before. And never in my wildest dreams had I expected to share my first experience with the guy I'd crushed on for years.

After I'd come down his throat, I was shocked when he didn't allow me to reciprocate. I couldn't wait until we were alone again, so I could do more than jerk him off. Although, I wasn't going to complain about using my hands on him to make him feel good, like he had done for me.

When my alarm went off the next morning, I was exhausted, but I had to get up for school. As I got ready, I couldn't stop staring at the moon tattoo on my wrist. I couldn't believe Malachi had been willing to mark himself permanently to help put me at ease since I'd been nervous. Knowing we had matching tattoos meant something to me, but I knew better than to read too much into things. He'd already told me no one could find out about us.

It didn't take me long to get dressed and head to school. The moment I stepped onto campus, my buddy AJ rushed over and pulled me aside.

"I need you to help me work on a poster to ask Daisy to winter formal," he said, sounding out of breath.

Daisy was the girl my friend had wanted to ask out for months, but he hadn't built up the courage to do it yet. And for some reason, everyone thought they needed to make some huge gesture just to get a date for a dance.

"Isn't the dance almost two months away? Why are you so worried about it now?" I asked.

"Her friend, Alexandria, said she found the perfect dress but didn't want to buy it before she had a date. I figured now might be a good time to ask her."

I nodded. "Okay. I don't know how much help I'll be, but we can work on something after school."

"Thanks, man. I owe you one." The bell rang, and we began walking to our first class. "You should come with us. Xavier and Dominic were talking about us going as a group and renting a limo."

"I probably won't have a date, though." There was only one person I wanted to take, but that wasn't a possibility.

"Who cares? It's senior year, and you shouldn't miss out on anything."

I shrugged. "I'll think about it."

"Nice tattoo by the way. Did you get that done yesterday?"

"Thanks," I replied. "And yeah, it was a birthday gift from my brother."

"What made you pick a moon?"

"I wasn't sure what to get and thought it looked cool," I lied because I couldn't tell him what it really meant to me.

As I headed to my car at the end of the day, I received a text from Malachi:

> Hey! Got any plans this afternoon?

> I'm supposed to help a friend with a project. Why?

> Well, I know Jesse's at work and no one is going to be at my place. Thought you might want to come over

"What's that smile for?" AJ asked as he suddenly appeared.

"Nothing. Someone just sent me a funny meme." I shoved my phone into my pocket. "So, how long do you think it will take this afternoon?"

A part of me hoped it would be quick, but then I felt like a shitty friend for wanting to ditch AJ so I could see Malachi.

"Not long. Dominic gave me a good idea for the wording, so I just need your help with the decorating. Shouldn't take more than an hour."

"Okay. Are we hitting up the store first to get the shit you need?"

He nodded. "Yeah. Figured you could follow me and then we can head over to my house."

"Sounds good."

I got into my car and fired off a text to Malachi:

> I'll be over in about an hour

> See you then

ONCE I WAS DONE HELPING AJ, I SPED HOME, PULLED INTO MY driveway, and hurried to my room to drop off my backpack and freshen up a bit, before walking down the street to Malachi's house. I barely managed to knock before the door flung open and I was pulled inside.

"Someone seems happy to see me," I teased as he kicked the door closed behind us.

"Yeah, well, I was getting impatient." He smiled and led me upstairs. "What were you doing, anyway?"

"My friend wanted help asking a girl to winter formal."

We stepped inside his room, and he locked the door behind us. "Ah. I remember it being stressful coming up with a creative way to do that."

I snorted. "Like you needed to do anything special. The ladies were practically tripping over themselves for you to notice them."

He guided me to sit on his bed. "What can I say? The whole lead singer thing has its advantages."

"You're ridiculous." I shook my head even though he wasn't wrong. On several occasions, I had witnessed how much attention he got for being the front man of Surrender.

"So, you were helping your friend. Are you going too?" He placed his hand on my leg and began stroking my thigh.

Whenever he touched me, it became difficult to think, but I managed to answer him, anyway. "I'm not sure. My friends want to do a whole group thing."

"You should go," he said, leaning over and kissing my neck.

"We'll see," I replied breathlessly. "But there's something else I'd rather be doing right now than talking about some school dance."

He smirked. "And what's that?"

I slid off the bed and crawled between his legs. "Last night, you gave me a birthday gift to remember, and now it's my turn to give you something back."

The next couple of months continued with Malachi and me sneaking around to meet up whenever we could. Unfortunately, it wasn't as often as either of us would have liked.

While I was busy with school and my weekend job at the diner, Malachi and the band had completed their virtual audition for *The Band Showdown* and were playing as many gigs as possible.

Before I knew it, it was time for winter formal. As I finished getting ready, I took a selfie in the bathroom mirror and sent it to Malachi. His response came quickly.

> Looking good. Now I'm worried about other guys hitting on you tonight

> Thanks. But there's no reason to be worried. I've got my hands full with you

> You got that right

A row of smirking emojis followed his text, and I couldn't help but laugh. The guy was cocky, but honestly, he had every right to be.

I tucked my phone into the pocket of my dress pants and went to the living room, where my parents were waiting to take a few pictures of me.

"Ah, sweetie, you look great." My mother clasped her hands together and smiled.

"Thanks, Mom." I hugged her and then moved in front of the fireplace so Dad could snap photos.

Once they were done, I headed out to my car and drove to AJ's house, where our group was meeting up.

It took an hour to get through another round of parents taking pictures, and then we were on our way to the hotel where the dance was being held.

"Oh my god, this looks so cool," Daisy squealed when we entered the ballroom.

The space was decorated in blue, silver, and white, making it look as though a snowstorm had blown through. A deejay was set up on the stage, playing some current hits as our classmates filled the dance floor.

"Let's get something to drink, and then we can dance," Xavier suggested, and we walked over to the tables with snacks, a hot chocolate station, and sodas on them.

I grabbed a can of Coke and turned to look at the crowd. It seemed like everyone was having a good time, and while I was happy to be hanging out with my friends, I couldn't help but think I would have more fun if I was with Malachi.

"Drink up." AJ bumped me with his shoulder. "We're ready to dance."

I downed my soda and then followed our group to the dance floor. I stayed out there as long as I could, but eventually, I needed a break and headed back to get another drink and a snack. As I reached for a cookie, I felt my phone vibrate. Slipping it out of my pocket, I looked at the screen and saw a message from Malachi:

> Come meet me in room 932 when you're done

I had to read the text several times before it sank in that he was at the hotel. At my winter formal. Asking me to join him in a room upstairs.

Not wanting to waste a single second, I rushed to the lobby and pressed the button for the elevator. While I waited, I texted AJ:

> Not feeling well. I'm going to have a rideshare pick me up

The elevator doors slid open, and I stepped inside. I pressed the button for the ninth floor and leaned against the back wall as I tried to calm my racing heart.

I could only imagine one reason why someone would book a hotel room and ask the person they were messing around with on a regular basis to join them.

We hadn't had sex yet, but I felt I was ready to take that step if that was what he wanted as well. Still, I was slightly nervous. If the rumors were true, Malachi had a decent amount of experience, and I didn't want him to be disappointed.

Before I could get lost in my thoughts, my phone buzzed with another notification.

> AJ: That sucks. Do you want me to wait with you?

> Nah. The car is a few minutes away

I hated lying to my friend, but I couldn't tell him that the guy I was secretly dating had surprised me by showing up tonight.

When the elevator reached the ninth floor, I walked off and followed the signs down the hallway that led to the room Malachi was waiting in. Lifting my hand, I knocked and waited for Malachi. When the door swung open, his eyes widened in surprise. "Hey. I wasn't sure if you got my message. You didn't respond."

"That's because I was in too much of a hurry to get up here."

"I didn't mean for you to leave the dance early. I just wanted you to know I was here whenever you were done."

"Trust me, there's nowhere else I'd rather be." I placed my hands on the sides of his face and crushed my lips to his. He opened for me, and our tongues tangled together while I slipped my hands under his T-shirt, gliding over every ridge of his well-defined body.

When we broke apart to catch our breaths, he rested his forehead against mine. "You know, I didn't invite you up here just to attack you the second you stepped inside."

I quirked an eyebrow and grinned. "Are you sure about that? I don't know anyone who would get a hotel room only to hang out."

He chuckled. "True, but I promise there's no pressure. I really did just want to spend time with you after your dance. You're in control of whatever happens tonight."

While I appreciated him taking into consideration what I was comfortable doing, I was more than ready to take the next step.

"I don't want to wait any longer."

He groaned and attacked my mouth again. "You look sexy as fuck, but you have too many clothes on." He pushed my suit jacket down my arms.

While he worked the buttons on my dress shirt, I ripped his T-shirt over his head. We couldn't keep our hands off each other as we moved toward the bed. I kicked off my shoes, pulling Malachi on top of me as I laid down. His lips burned a path down my neck, across my chest, and to the waistband of my pants.

Looking up at me, he smirked as he worked my fly and stripped me out of my slacks and boxers. Once I lay naked on the bed, a hint of nervousness washed over me as I anticipated his next move.

"Have you done this before?" he asked, massaging my inner thighs.

I shook my head. "You're my first. What about you?" He gave me a look as though I had asked the most ridiculous question because he knew that I knew he wasn't a virgin. "I mean with a guy."

"Ah." He moved down further between my spread legs. "No. I've never had sex with a guy before."

"Really?" Based on how he took control when we messed around, I'd assumed he had his fair share of experience with men as well as women.

He nodded. "I haven't done much with guys until you."

The idea we were sharing our first experience filled me with happiness, and the nerves I had been feeling a moment ago faded away.

Malachi grasped the base of my dick and licked me from root to tip. My hips bucked, desperate for more.

"If you don't like anything I do, I need you to let me know."

I nodded.

"I need to hear your words, Jasper."

My eyes met his. "Okay. I'll tell you."

Seemingly happy with my answer, he wrapped his lips around my crown and pumped my shaft with his fist. My fingers twisted in the sheets as I enjoyed the pleasure his hot mouth was giving me. Just as I felt myself on the edge of coming, he pulled off my cock and opened the duffle bag I hadn't noticed on the bed. Digging around, he removed a condom, which he tossed next to me, then grabbed a bottle of lube, flipped the cap open, and poured a generous amount onto his fingers. He pushed my legs further apart with his other hand and engulfed my cock once more.

One of his cool, wet digits began tracing my rim, and a low groan escaped my lips.

"Has anyone ever touched you here?" he asked.

"I've done it myself a few times when jerking off, but no one else has," I admitted.

"The thought of you fingering your ass while stroking your dick is fucking hot." He slowly pressed the tip of his finger inside me while swirling his tongue over my shaft like a popsicle. He added another digit, scissoring them a bit to stretch my hole.

"Give me more, please," I begged.

He pushed in a third, and the slight burn had me squirming against him.

"Just breathe. I'll go slow."

I let out a breath like he instructed. "Okay."

He took his time pumping in and out of me, and my body melted into his touch.

"God, I want to fuck you so bad."

"Then do it," I urged.

He slid off the bed, stepped out of his sweats, then crawled back between my legs. He sat back on his heels, ripped open the foil packet, and rolled the condom down his considerable length. I watched as he coated himself in the slick gel before he hooked his arms under my legs and lined himself up with my needy asshole.

As he eased his dick inside me, my eyes slammed shut. He gave me a moment to adjust to the new sensation, then leaned down and brushed my lips with his. "You're squeezing the hell out of my dick. It feels so fucking good. Tell me when you're ready for me to move."

I wrapped my arms around his neck, kissing him once more before I said, "Go ahead. I'm ready."

He rocked into me with long, slow strokes. Once I allowed myself to relax, it didn't take long for the discomfort to morph into pleasure. My knees fell open, allowing him to go even deeper; all the while his lips never left mine, his tongue plunging into my mouth.

When he pulled back, he wrapped his hand around my dick and pumped it in time with his thrusts. "Watching you take my cock is the sexiest thing I've ever seen."

"Shit, that feels so good," I moaned. My release continued building, and with a few more jerks, I came all over his fist and my stomach.

He groaned and picked up the pace. "Fuck, I'm going to come too."

He pounded into me two more times, then stilled as he spilled into the condom.

He hovered over me and captured my mouth in another kiss. "That was fucking amazing."

At that moment, I knew I was falling in love with Malachi Danvers.

6

MALACHI

If my best friend found out I fucked his brother, everything would turn to shit. Not only was I certain Jesse would drug me and cut my dick off while I was sleeping, but he would never speak to me again. At least, that was what I assumed, because if I were to find out he was fucking my sister, I would do exactly those things. It was bro code, and I went and broke it by falling hard for Jasper. So hard that I was sneaking around kissing him, getting matching tattoos with him, blowing him, and now reserving a hotel room for the night so I could fuck him.

Who was I?

I wouldn't have said I was *in* love with him, though I certainly had love *for* him. I cared so much about him not only because I was attracted to him, but because I'd known Jasper almost his entire life. He was funny and smart, could whip up gourmet meals, and was an amazing person. I never thought any of what we were doing would happen.

But I was happy.

However, in the back of my mind, I knew if the band and I made it to the live auditions for *The Band Showdown* and then won, everything would change.

Except, I couldn't keep my hands off of him.

We lay in the middle of the king-sized hotel bed after we cleaned up and slipped on our boxers. I pulled him closer to me and traced my finger over the moon tattoo on his wrist. When I glanced at the clock on the nightstand, I saw it was almost midnight.

"Where do your parents think you are?" I mumbled against his shoulder, and kissed it lightly.

"My friend, AJ's. The plan was to go there after the after-party."

"And stay the night there?"

"Yeah." He nodded.

I rose up and rolled until I was on top of him. "So, we get to stay all night like this?"

His grin matched mine. "If you want."

"Hell yeah, I do, but are you hungry?"

"I could eat."

I reached over and grabbed my cell from the nightstand. Pulling up the delivery app, I scrolled through the options.

"We could order pizza or Chinese, or maybe even room service?" I suggested.

"Whatever you want, it's cool with me. I ate before the dance, but I kinda worked up an appetite since then." Jasper grinned.

I had too. "Fuck it. Room service will be faster and after we eat, I can have my way with you again."

We stared at each other for a beat, more than likely both of us thinking we could wait to order food, but I cleared my throat and went to get the menu. Jasper was probably too sore to fuck again, but I had other ideas.

We flipped through the small menu and settled on burgers and fries, but when I called, I was told they were closed for the night.

"Room service ended at 10." I blew out a breath.

"Belle's is open twenty-four hours," he said about the diner where he worked. "We can get it delivered."

"Yeah, but the best chef isn't working tonight." I grinned at him.

He snorted a laugh. "I just prep the food mostly."

"Still my favorite chef." I winked. "But okay, let's get it delivered."

After I placed the order for burgers and fries, we leaned against the headboard and I flipped through the TV channels.

"So, how was the dance?" I asked, not finding anything worth watching on the limited number of stations.

He lifted a shoulder. "It was okay. Nothing too exciting."

"Did you dance?"

"Of course."

"With another dude?"

Jasper cut his eyes to me. "With my straight friends. Are you jealous?"

"No, not really. I mean, I would have loved to have danced with you."

"Do you wanna dance now?"

He asked as though he were joking, but the thought made me happy. "Yeah, let's dance."

"Really?" he gasped as I slid off the bed.

I went around to his side and held out my hand. "Yep, really."

"But there's no music playing," he protested.

I cocked my head slightly. "Do we need any?"

I knew I could easily play something on my phone, but that wasn't what I wanted to do in that moment.

He shook his head and took my hand. I led him to the open space at the end of the bed and sang the lyrics to an older song my parents played often. It was their wedding song, and I had no idea why the song came to me while I had Jasper in my arms, but since I loved the raspiness of the singer's voice, I went with it.

"What song is this?" Jasper asked as I sang about how, if he looked into my eyes, he would see what he meant to me. If he searched his heart and his soul, he would find me there and he wouldn't have to search anymore.

""Everything I Do" by Bryan Adams."

"I like it. Keep going," he said as we swayed side to side, only dressed in our boxers.

And I did. I sang all the words while we moved together. I twirled him a few times, and as the song ended, I kissed him.

"I guess it's true," he said when we pulled apart.

"What's that?"

"You can sing the panties off of chicks."

I snorted a laugh. "I've never sung that song to anyone else."

"Yeah, well, I bet you could sing the alphabet and it would work."

Jasper pushed me back until my legs hit the end of the bed and, without another word, he pulled my boxers down. I sucked in a small breath, watching as he sank to his knees and looked up at me with his intoxicating blue eyes.

He fisted my hardening dick, giving it a few pumps before licking the crown. "You taste so good."

I groaned at his words and threaded my fingers through his dirty blond hair, guiding his head as he engulfed my length. My knees felt as though they were going to give out, so I slowly sank until I was sitting on the bed. Never once did he take his greedy mouth off my cock as he moved with me. Instead, once I was seated, he went faster, sucking and bobbing as his hand worked my base at the same time.

"Fuck, that feels so good," I praised, watching as his mouth slid up and down my shaft. "If you don't slow down, I'm going to come down your throat any second."

He looked up at me with hooded eyes and mumbled around the tip. "Do it."

My balls tightened at his demand and within seconds, I was shooting my jizz into his warm, wet mouth. He swallowed it all and once I was spent, he sat back on his heels and wiped his lips with the back of his hand.

"Damn. I'm so glad I got this hotel room for us." I reached for him and he grabbed my hand.

"Me too."

Pulling him up, he got onto the bed beside me and I hooked my leg over his hip as we lay face to face. Without thinking or caring about how I had just come in his mouth, I leaned forward and kissed him. He opened and our tongues swirled together, giving me a taste of my cum. Fuck, it was amazing.

He was amazing.

I was about to slide down his body so I could make him come with my mouth, but there was a knock at the door. It was time for actual food.

A FEW HOURS LATER, THE ALARM ON MY PHONE WENT OFF AN HOUR before I needed to check out of the hotel. We hadn't slept much. After we'd eaten our burgers and fooled around again, we finally fell asleep. I was pretty certain by the time we fell asleep, the sun had started to come up, which was just a few hours ago.

"Already?" Jasper groaned.

"We have an hour, but yeah," I replied as I shut the alarm off.

"Well, I know what I'll be doing today." He rolled onto his back.

"Sleeping?"

"For sure."

I sat up. "The guys and I are practicing at your house."

"Of course you are." He chuckled.

"What? You don't want me there?" I teased.

He looked up at me. "I'd rather you be in my bedroom than the garage."

"Trust me." I leaned down and kissed him. "I'd like that too."

"Maybe tonight you can sneak in after everyone goes to sleep?"

"I can do that."

We both climbed out of the bed and started to get dressed.

"Do you need a ride home?" I asked, stepping into my jeans.

"Actually, my car is at AJ's. Can you drop me off there?"

"Sure."

Once in my Jeep, I cranked the engine, and "Cardigan" by Taylor Swift was already playing on the satellite station. I started singing the lyrics as I reversed out of the parking spot in the hotel's garage and headed toward the street.

"I had no idea you liked Taylor Swift," Jasper stated.

"What's wrong with Taylor Swift?" I grinned and looked over at him.

"Nothing. Go on."

I did as he wanted, singing softly about a first love and the first heartbreak that went along with it, and when the song was over, he said, "Wow. I know you have an amazing voice, but damn, it really is beautiful."

"Thank you."

"I'm so used to hearing it with the rest of Surrender, but listening to you sing like this, just you and the music playing quietly, it's ... different."

I chuckled. "Well, maybe I'll have to serenade you more often."

"Maybe you should," he replied with a grin.

As we approached AJ's house, I slowed down and pulled over a few houses away. "Here we are."

Jasper unbuckled his seatbelt. "Thanks for the ride."

"Anytime." I smiled, leaning over to give him a quick kiss. "I'll see you back at your place later, okay?"

"Definitely. Looking forward to it."

I watched him get into his car, then I sighed happily and drove off, Taylor Swift's voice still playing in my head. I was on a high after the night we'd had and I wished we could be together every night. Just me and Jasper, but sadly, it couldn't be that way.

I WAS BELTING OUT THE LYRICS TO "BENT" BY BUCKCHERRY AS WE jammed out in Jesse's garage. I tried not to think about Jasper being inside the house asleep in his bed and the fact I wanted to walk inside and crawl in next to him.

As the song ended, I grabbed my energy drink and finished it. After the night before and this morning, I felt like I needed five highly caffeinated beverages to survive until it was time to go home and climb into my own bed. I had no idea when that would be, because I was honestly counting down the minutes until I could sneak into Jasper's room again.

Jesse grabbed his phone off the coffee table and plopped onto the beat-up sofa. I assumed he was texting with Olivia until he said, "Guys …" We all looked at him. "We did it. We made it to the live auditions in LA!"

All of us jumped up, screaming and celebrating with bro hugs and huge ass smiles. Holy shit, we were going to California!

"When do we leave?" Elliott asked.

Jesse looked back at his phone and then said, "Right after the new year."

That was in a few weeks.

"That soon?" I questioned.

"Yeah, man," he replied. "We're about to have a crazy few months, at least. More if we fucking win."

"*When* we win," Silas stated. "We're fucking winning."

"Hell yeah!" Elliott and Silas high-fived.

A few months of us in LA, while Jasper's back in Boston. The realization hit me hard. There would be no sneaking around. No kissing. No touching. No seeing him every day, and I knew deep down I was going to miss him like crazy.

"You good?" Jesse clapped me on the back.

"Yep." I nodded and plastered on a smile, despite my internal thoughts. "Just can't believe it."

"Well, fucking believe it! We need to go tell everyone."

Tell everyone … Tell Jasper.

Shit.

"Let me get my parents over here so we can let everyone know together." I pulled my phone out of my pocket.

"I'm going to head home and share the news with my parents," Silas stated.

"Me too," Elliott said.

Our friends left, and I dialed my mom.

"Hey, honey," she answered.

"Hey. Can you and Dad come down to Jesse's?" I asked.

"Is everything okay?" she questioned.

I nodded and looked at Jesse with finally a genuine smile. "Things are amazing. We have news."

She gasped. "You made it to the live auditions?"

"Just come over." I chuckled.

"We'll be right there."

I hung up and followed Jesse into his house.

"Fam," he yelled. "Come to the kitchen!"

"What's going on?" his dad asked, coming into the room.

His mom was right behind him, but I didn't see Jasper. He was probably sound asleep with earplugs in, so he couldn't hear us practicing. I didn't blame him.

"You'll find out in a second. We're waiting for Mal's parents, and where the hell is Jasper?" Jesse questioned.

"In his room," Mrs. B replied. "Does this mean Surrender is going to LA?"

Before Jesse could confirm we were, there was a knock on the front door.

"I'll get it," I said.

"I'll go get Jasper." Jesse walked down the hall toward his brother's room while I went to the front door.

"Well?" Mom asked as I swung the door open.

My face still had a huge ass smile on it, but I didn't confirm their suspicions. "Just come in. We're waiting on Jasper."

Mom and Dad stepped into the house and followed me into the kitchen, where Jesse's parents were still waiting. Jasper finally emerged from his room, his tousled hair and sleepy eyes a stark contrast to the excitement buzzing around us.

"So?" Jesse's mom questioned.

Jesse and I shared a quick look and then we said together, "We're going to LA!"

The room erupted in cheers and congratulations with hugs for my friend and me. When my eyes locked with Jasper's, he gave me a tight smile and I knew he was thinking the same thing I was: Would there still be an us?

We stepped together and hugged.

"Congrats," he said.

I didn't want to let him go, but I did and moved a step back. "Thank you."

"We leave the first week of January," Jesse said to whomever wanted to know.

"You leave that soon?" Jasper asked.

I nodded. "Guess so."

I was pulled away and into a hug by his mom. When I broke free of her, Jasper had disappeared. I slipped down the hall to his room, knocking softly before pushing the door open to find him sitting on the edge of his bed.

"Hey," I said softly, my heart breaking with the pain radiating off of him as I closed the door behind me.

Looking up, his eyes met mine. Without a word, I crossed the room and sat beside him, our shoulders touching as we stared down at the hardwood floor in front of us. And though we didn't speak, the silence between us spoke volumes, a bittersweet reminder that the months we had secretly shared were coming to an end.

As the minutes ticked by, I wished for nothing more than to freeze time, to hold on to that moment, but my dream was always to make it big and this was the break Surrender needed. I couldn't jeopardize it for whatever was between me and Jasper.

"I really am happy for you," Jasper finally whispered.

"I know."

"But it didn't hit me until now that you'd be leaving for a few months."

"Me too." I placed my hand on his knee.

"But you have to go."

"I do."

The room felt suffocating as we sat there, coping with reality. I could hear our parents and Jesse down the hall, still on a high, as they talked about LA and what was to come.

"I wish …" Jasper's voice trailed off, his gaze still on the floor in front of us.

"I know," I whispered. "But maybe we won't even make it past the live audition."

He snorted. "We both know that's not true. You guys are amazing."

"But we don't know how the competition will go."

"True, but something is telling me this is going to be your big moment."

I swallowed. "Me too."

I turned slightly and brushed my fingers against his cheek. I was seconds away from kissing him, but then I heard Jesse yell, "Malachi! Where did you go? We're going out for steak and lobster to celebrate!"

With a heavy sigh, I stood. "I better slip out before your brother finds me in here."

"Guess I need to get dressed for dinner too."

"Yeah. We can talk more tonight, okay?"

"What is there to talk about?" His gaze finally lifted to mine. "We'll just have to see what happens, right?"

"Right." I blew out a breath.

"But no matter what, I'll miss you."

I reached for him, making him stand, and wrapping my arms around him. "I'll miss you too."

Without another thought, I kissed him so he knew I meant it.

7

Jasper

"What are you doing here?" I twisted the lock on my bedroom door, locking us inside.

Malachi stood from where he had been sitting on the edge of my bed and stalked toward me. "Your window was unlocked, and I needed to see you one more time before I leave tomorrow."

The weeks since the guys found out they were headed to LA had passed so fast, Malachi and I had hardly had a moment to ourselves. And when we had been together, we'd both avoided talking about what his leaving meant for us. Deep down, I knew we really had no future. Our lives were headed in different directions, but that didn't mean my feelings for him hadn't grown stronger over the last few months while we'd been sneaking around.

"You're lucky Jesse isn't here."

"He told me he was going to the gym, so I knew it was safe."

"I can't believe this is the last time I'm going to see you for a while." I cupped the back of his neck and pulled him in for a kiss.

"I can't believe it either," he said against my lips. "I didn't expect it to be so hard to say goodbye."

Slowly, I walked us back toward my bed, and we tumbled onto the mattress when his knees hit the edge. Straddling his thighs, I reached for the button of his jeans. I wanted nothing more than to be with him one more time.

We were lying breathless on my bed when someone tried to open my door, but it wouldn't budge since it was locked.

Jesse knocked. "Jasper, open up?"

"You've got to be kidding me," I grumbled, and then said louder, "What do you want?"

"Did you forget we were supposed to go get pizza tonight?"

Yeah, I had forgotten, even though I'd been excited a couple of days ago when we planned to spend a little *brother time* together before he left.

"I remembered," I lied. "Just give me a sec."

Malachi climbed out of bed and threw on his clothes.

"I wish you didn't have to leave." I sighed.

"Me too, but you should go have fun with Jesse," he whispered and headed to the window.

Before he climbed out, I pressed my lips to his one final time. "Good luck in LA."

I may have wanted more time with him, but maybe this was the perfect way to say goodbye. We had gotten some time together without another depressing conversation about this being the end for us. Our situation, whatever it was, had always been temporary and now it was over. But that didn't mean my heart wasn't breaking knowing we'd never share these moments again.

"Thanks." He looked like he wanted to say more, but Jesse knocked again.

"Jasper, seriously, what are you doing?"

Once I was sure Malachi was gone, I opened the door. "Sorry. I'm ready now."

"Why do you sound out of breath? Did I interrupt you jerking off or something?" He laughed.

"You're ridiculous." I tried to play it off as a joke, even though he wasn't too far from the truth. "I'm definitely not going to miss your childish sense of humor while you're gone."

"Sure, you will. But don't worry, little brother, I won't forget about you when I'm a star."

Maybe he wouldn't, but I wasn't so sure the same could be said about his best friend.

THE NEXT MORNING BEFORE SCHOOL, MY PARENTS AND I SAID OUR goodbyes to Jesse. Olivia was dropping him off at the airport where he was meeting up with the rest of Surrender to fly to LA.

"Gonna miss you, kid." Jesse slapped my back playfully.

"Me too."

He might have gotten on my nerves at times, especially when he thought he knew more than me or was overprotective, but the two of us were as close as brothers could be, and it was going to be strange not seeing him every day.

"You've got everything you need?" Mom asked for probably the hundredth time.

Jesse snorted. "Yeah, Mom. I even checked the tracking on the stuff I shipped ahead, and it should all be delivered tomorrow."

"Okay, but let us know if you need anything else." Tears shone in her eyes.

"I will." He kissed her cheek.

"Good luck out there, Son. We'll be rooting for you." Dad pulled him in for a hug.

"Thanks," he replied.

After our mom fussed over him a little more, he grabbed his two suitcases and guitar and followed Olivia to her car. My parents and I stood on the porch, and we watched as they drove off.

Once the car was out of sight, I walked inside, and headed toward my room to grab my phone.

> Me: Have you left yet?

> Malachi: Yeah. I can't believe this is actually happening

> I'll be watching you on TV and then I'll see you at the finale

> Don't jinx it 😊

I could understand why he didn't want to come across as overconfident about their chances of winning, but I'd watched other seasons of *The Band Showdown* and knew they were just as good, if not better, than previous winners.

> Malachi: I'm really going to miss you

> I'll miss you too

I put my phone down and began getting ready for school. Hopefully, my classes and my friends would help keep my mind off of Malachi and how sad I was that we'd never really had a shot.

AT THE END OF THE DAY, I WAS STILL IN A FUNK, SO AFTER FINISHING my homework, I started preparing dinner. I had just finished assembling a pan of enchiladas when my mom came home. She placed her bag on the chair at the island and hugged me.

"Hi, sweetie. How was school today?"

"It was fine," I replied and moved to put the enchiladas in the oven.

"Your brother texted me a few minutes ago. They made it to LA."

"Oh … That's good." It was probably silly of me to be disappointed that Mom told me instead of finding out from Malachi by a text.

She frowned. "Are you okay?"

"Yeah. Why?"

"You just seem a bit down. I know not having Jesse around will be a big adjustment, but if they make it to the end, you'll be so busy with all of your senior year stuff you'll hardly notice he's gone. Then June will be here before you know it, and we can see him again."

I couldn't tell her it wasn't my brother who I was missing so much. Instead, I agreed with her. "I'm sure you're right."

While I started some rice, she walked to the fridge, grabbed a bottle of white wine, and poured herself a glass.

"Speaking of senior year, have you thought any more about what you want to do after graduation? I know you were looking at courses at Bunker Hill, and registration opens soon."

My plan was to attend our local community college and then maybe transfer to Hawkins University after two years. However, with Jesse off chasing his dream, it made me realize I didn't really have one of my own.

"A little bit, but I don't know what I want to do yet."

"Well, I happened to come across an ad for culinary school on social media today."

I tilted my head. "How'd that show up on your timeline?"

She chuckled. "I'd told my boss about the incredible braised short ribs you made the other day. You know those apps are always listening."

I nodded because my feeds were full of cooking videos and ads for bakeware. "It's kind of creepy."

"It is." She took a sip of wine. "But the program has a lot to offer. The school offers cuisine and pastry courses, and you'd get to live in Paris while doing something you love. I know you said you wanted to go to Europe one day."

Paris would be exciting, and making a career out of something I was passionate about would be awesome. "That actually sounds really cool. Can you send me the info?"

She smiled. "Absolutely."

I sat in the living room and worked on some homework while waiting for *The Band Showdown* to start. It had been three months since the guys had left for LA, and I still missed Malachi like crazy.

At first, he and I texted several times a week, but once they started filming the live shows a few weeks ago, more time seemed to pass between messages. My head and heart were in a constant battle. Not having him around all the time and sharing secret moments hurt even more than I expected. But I tried to remember how the competition was a once-in-a-lifetime opportunity for him and my brother, and was where his focus needed to be.

I was barely paying attention to the TV until the host, Kirk Benson, announced it was time for Surrender to perform. The second Malachi started singing "Natural" by Imagine Dragons, the audience went wild. He moved around the stage effortlessly while giving the impression he was singing directly to those in the crowd, proving he was born to be a star.

"I don't know how it's possible, but they sound better and better every week." Mom beamed.

"There's no way they aren't making it to the finale," Dad said.

"None of the other bands even come close to how good they are," I added.

As they finished their performance, I felt the familiar ache in my chest that came with the reminder that it would be another week before I could watch him again. And I often wondered if I would ever get over the sadness of losing him.

While the show went to commercial, I decided to check my email. In my inbox was an email I'd been waiting on for a couple of weeks. Clicking to open it, I read the first line.

"Holy crap," I breathed.

"Everything okay?" my mom asked.

"Uh … yeah. Everything's fine."

Dad lifted an eyebrow. "Then what's going on?"

"I got into the Paris culinary school."

TWO MONTHS LATER, I SAT WITH MY PARENTS IN THE AUDIENCE OF *THE BAND SHOWDOWN*. Surrender had made it to the finale with two other groups, and we would soon find out if they won.

From the moment the cameras started rolling, everything moved quickly. When it was time for Surrender to perform for the last time on the show, we, along with the other guys' families and Olivia, were directed to sit in the front row. It had been the same when the other bands were on stage. It allowed the production crew to get clear shots of us cheering for our loved ones.

Kirk Benson stood center stage and introduced the guys. "And now for the night's final performance, welcome back to the stage, Surrender."

The entire studio erupted in applause as the lights went down. A second later, the sound of Jesse's guitar filled the venue. As the intro faded out, a spotlight illuminated Malachi standing in the center of the stage, one hand wrapped around the mic stand and the other pushing his dark brown hair off his gorgeous face.

He looked out at the crowd and began singing as Elliott and Silas joined in with Jesse. On the surface, Malachi looked like the same guy who had left months ago, but he seemed to have gained even more confidence since he'd been on the show. He was made for the stage.

I continued to watch as he poured every possible emotion into his lyrics. If I'd been a better brother, I would have spent an equal amount of time paying attention to Jesse, but I couldn't tear my gaze away from Malachi. His voice was deep and smooth and hearing it again in person caused goosebumps to form along my skin. All of those feelings I had tried to bury over the past few months rose to the surface again, and it hurt to know our lives were going in different directions.

Their song came to an end far too quickly. When it was time for the winner to be announced, the anticipation was killing me. I couldn't imagine how it was for the guys.

Kirk Benson returned to the stage with an envelope in his hand. "It's the moment you've all been waiting for. These final three bands have endured countless hours of practice and performances, all in the hope of being named the next winner of *The Band Showdown*. After tallying the votes, we're ready to announce the band whose dreams are about to come true."

The lights dimmed once again, and the house band started a drum roll.

"The winner of this year's *The Band Showdown* is ..."

My heart felt as though it had stopped in my chest as we all stared at the stage. I was nervous for my brother and Malachi as we waited the seconds that felt like an eternity for Kirk to utter the words we wanted to hear.

"Surrender!"

I jumped to my feet along with my parents, Olivia, the Danvers, and Silas's and Elliott's families as we shouted and clapped.

They had done it.

Once the cameras stopped rolling, we were ushered backstage. Dozens of people surrounded the band, but the minute the guys saw all of us, they came rushing over.

"Holy shit! Can you believe it?" Jesse wrapped his arms around all of us.

"We're so proud of you," Mom gushed.

"You were incredible," Dad added.

I smiled. "I knew from the beginning you were going to win."

We continued to celebrate, and eventually, Malachi made his way to me.

"Congratulations." I gave him a hug. "You looked amazing out there."

"Thank you. It's been a wild ride," he replied.

"Yeah, Jesse's been sending me pics. Looks like you guys have been living your best life."

He frowned slightly and lowered his voice. "About that. I'm sorry I haven't texted much."

I shook my head. "You don't have to explain. We both knew things would change once you were out here."

Even though I'd had a difficult time dealing with his absence, I didn't want him to feel bad.

"I'd really like to talk—"

"Surrender, we need you all over here for some pictures," an assistant called out.

"Later, okay?"

I nodded and watched Malachi walk away once again. Before we'd arrived, we had been told that if they won, they were obligated to do photoshoots and interviews immediately following the show, so even though I agreed we could catch up later, I knew we wouldn't have any time alone because I was leaving the next day for Paris.

8

MALACHI

Three and a Half Years Later – Present Day

The intrusive sun pierced through the crack in my drapes that I'd failed to close correctly. The guys and I were spending long hours in the studio as we recorded our new album "Neon Nights," which was due to be released the first of the year, after which we would go on tour in the spring to promote it. I was used to staying up all night and sleeping all day, but not when the sun and drapes were working against me.

Groaning, I rolled over and checked the time. I thought I still had a few hours until my alarm was set to go off, but to my surprise, I only had a few more minutes until it was time to get up. My only motivation to get out of bed was knowing Savannah Sky was coming into the studio to record a duet our label had set up for the new album.

Life had been a rollercoaster ride since winning *The Band Showdown*. We went from performing for small crowds in bars near our hometown, to signing with Stellar Records, recording our first single, and hearing it on the radio! The track was a hit, and that led to our first album. It had been a whirlwind of appearances on talk shows, photoshoots for magazines, and performing for thousands at events and festivals. A year after we won the competition, we were the opening act for another band, which gave us a small taste of life on the road. Now we were going to be the headliners for a tour that would take us to more than thirty cities across the US and Canada.

It was going to be epic.

And exhausting.

But so, so worth it.

THE STUDIO BUZZED WITH ACTIVITY AS I STEPPED INSIDE.

"Finally, you arrive, Sleeping Beauty," Jesse greeted with a grin.

I flipped him the bird. "Not all of us have a wife who nags us to make sure we're on time."

Jesse and Olivia weren't married, but they might as well have been. They'd been together for over six years, and she pretty much kept us all alive.

"Don't be mad because you wake up alone every morning," Jesse teased.

"That's how I like it, thank you very much."

"Yeah, none of us want to be tied down like you," Silas stated, giving me a bro hug.

"Trust me, when you fuckers fall in love, you'll understand," Jesse retorted.

Elliott walked into the room with Savannah Sky on his heels. I'd never met Savannah before, but Stellar Records wanted us to collaborate, so here we were, recording the final song for Surrender's album together.

"Why are we talking about love?" Silas asked.

I ignored my friends and stuck out my hand for Savannah. "Hey. I'm—"

"Malachi Danvers," she finished for me with a smile.

I grinned back as we shook. "Yep."

"Are we ready to do this?" Jesse probed.

"I'm ready," Savannah replied.

"Me too."

We walked into the adjacent room, which was separated from where the producers sat by a large window. Our mics were already set up with the lyrics printed and placed in front of us. As the guys got ready, I took a swig of water and read the words one last time.

"Which one of you wrote this song?" Savannah asked.

All eyes were on me as I lifted my hand. "That would be me."

"Oh wow. I love it."

"Thanks."

"Who's it about?"

Him. Always him.

"No one. The words just came to me one night," I lied.

With a nod, I indicated I was ready, and then Jesse got the signal from the producers and started to strum the melody. Silas and Elliott joined in, and when it was time, I began to sing ...

> *"In the darkness of the night, I feel your touch*
> *Though you're far away, my heart hasn't had enough*
> *Every whisper, every sigh, I keep dreaming of being by your side*
> *Wishing there was a way for us not to hide"*

Even though I was singing about someone else, I locked eyes with Savannah. Her voice was like velvet, weaving effortlessly with mine as I poured my soul into the words. She would smile at me, and I would grin back, and at some point, I felt as though we were singing to one another. I supposed that was what was meant to happen, but I wanted it to be *him*.

The music faded out, and even though we'd only done one take on the song, I felt as though we'd nailed it.

"Wow, Malachi," she breathed as she leaned in. "That was incredible."

I could feel the heat of her breath against my skin, which sent shivers down my spine. "Thanks, Savannah," I replied. "You were amazing too."

She chuckled. "You flatter me. But really, your lyrics speak to something deep inside. It's like you're singing straight from the soul."

I couldn't help but be drawn to her, the way her eyes sparkled. "Well, I guess I just write what I feel," I admitted.

Her gaze lingered on mine, her lips curving into a playful smile. "And what do you feel right now?"

I swallowed, suddenly feeling like I was caught in a whirlwind. I may have been thinking about someone else while singing, but I was still a man with needs. "Right now? I feel ... inspired. Inspired by your talent, your voice."

Her smile widened. "Well then, I'll take that as a compliment," she said, leaning in closer and running her finger down my chest. "But I must admit, there's something about you, Malachi Danvers. Something I want to get to know better."

I looked down at her finger and then back up to her eyes. "Maybe it's just the music bringing us together."

Savannah laughed softly and whispered, "Or maybe it's something more."

"All right. If you two are done," Jesse interrupted. "We need to re-record it."

ONCE WE WERE DONE, THE GUYS AND I PLUS SAVANNAH DECIDED TO GO out for drinks to celebrate. Savannah hadn't stopped flirting with me all day, and if things kept going the way they were, I wasn't going home alone after the club.

The city lights blurred as we sped toward West Hollywood. Jesse was behind the wheel of his Audi Q7 as he navigated through the streets of LA. We all decided to ride with Jesse and leave our cars at the studio for a few hours. Sandwiched between Elliott and me, Savannah's heat pressed against me. Silas was riding shotgun.

"You guys ready to dance?" Savannah asked over the music in the car.

"Absolutely," Elliott replied.

"And to hook up," Silas stated.

"I'll probably bail early and head home," Jesse said. "Can everyone find a ride later?"

"Sure." I waved him off. We were used to it since he tended not to spend much time away from Olivia.

Savannah leaned closer to me, her scent of jasmine and something sweet enveloping me. "I still can't believe we nailed that song. It was amazing."

"Yeah, it's always incredible hearing my songs come to life."

She flashed me a dazzling smile. "You know, I think we make a pretty good team."

"Definitely," I agreed, though I didn't want to add her to Surrender any time soon. She was a solo artist, and we had our own stuff. Plus, her vibe wasn't what we were about. She was more pop than rock.

When the car stopped outside the club, we could feel the bass pulsating through the air. Jesse turned off the engine and handed his keys to the valet. As we all stepped out onto the sidewalk, Savannah looped her arm through mine. I felt every eye on us as we walked toward the club's entrance and inside. I also wondered if the shadows hid any paparazzi just waiting to make a buck with a photo of me with yet *another* woman. It seemed to be all the news outlets talked about when my picture was taken out in public. Hell, I didn't blame them.

The dance floor was a sea of bodies, each person moving to the thumping beat. Jesse, Elliott, and Silas headed straight for the VIP section, leaving Savannah and me alone. She turned to me, her gaze locking with mine.

"Care to dance?" she asked, her voice barely audible over the music.

When I took her hand in mine, the connection sparked like wildfire.

"I thought you'd never ask," I replied, pulling her closer until our bodies were pressed together.

We danced song after song, and I leaned down and kissed her a time or two. She kissed me back, and after we were out of breath, we headed to the VIP area to join my friends.

"Got a bottle of vodka for the table," Jesse stated. "But I need to head out."

"We know." I laughed.

After he said his goodbyes, Silas headed to the restroom, and I poured Savannah, Elliott, and myself a round of shots.

"You two ever have a threesome?"

I choked at Savannah's question.

"Not with each other," Elliott answered with a chuckle.

"Would you ever?" she pressed.

While I was into guys, no one knew still—except the ones I hooked up with who signed a Non-Disclosure Agreement and *him*. It was better that way because of the band. I had an image to uphold, and I wasn't sure what would happen if someone saw me with a guy.

"I don't need to share," Elliott said. "A night with me, and you'll think I have more than two hands."

We were all laughing when Silas came back from the bathroom. He sniffed a few times, wiped his nose, and poured a shot. Elliott and I shared a look; we knew exactly what our bandmate was doing in the restroom.

"Oh my god!" Savannah shrieked before I could even think twice about what my friend had been up to.

She was holding her phone. "What?" I asked.

"Stellar Records wants me to go on tour with you guys."

"No way," I replied, unsure how I felt about it. However, we had cut a song together, so I supposed she could come out on stage for that one song.

"Yeah. They heard our song and loved it."

Our song. That song will never be mine and hers.

Every song I wrote was about *him*.

9

Jasper

Moving around my boss's state-of-the-art kitchen in his new condo, I put the final touches on the dinner I prepared. I'd finished culinary school in Paris two and a half years ago, and after spending some additional time in France, I had moved back home.

When I first returned to Boston, I worked at a couple of fine dining restaurants. However, I didn't enjoy it as much as I thought I would, and I decided to switch gears and became a personal chef. It gave me more creative control over the meals I cooked, and the hours were better too.

One of my clients was Sean Ashford, a top-rated criminal defense lawyer. Working for him was great because he didn't make many requests and liked anything I made. Due to his long work hours, I only needed to cook at his place a couple of times a week and pack away several meals he could heat up whenever he was home.

As I was cleaning up, I heard the front door open.

"Perfect timing, Sean. Dinner's ready." I turned around and was surprised to see his son, Ryan, instead. "Oh, hey. I didn't know you were eating with your father tonight."

He smiled. "I'm not. I just finished up a client meeting and wanted to use one of his parking spaces since I'm meeting up with some friends nearby, and parking is a bitch around here."

Parking within the city was nearly impossible. Any time I wasn't hauling groceries to a client's house, I preferred using public transportation instead of driving around the city—a habit I'd picked up while living in Europe. Thankfully, I'd already brought the food up to Sean's place earlier in the week, so a parking place remained open for Ryan.

"Makes sense."

"Are you expecting my dad to be home soon? I know one of his trials started recently."

I shook my head. "He's been working crazy hours. I haven't seen him at all for the last two weeks."

"So, we have the place to ourselves?" He grinned mischievously.

From the first time I'd made a family meal for Sean and his two adult children, Ryan had flirted with me whenever his dad wasn't looking. At first, I hadn't reciprocated because I didn't want to jeopardize my job. However, it didn't take long before I gave in. What could I say? The guy was fucking hot with his light brown hair and smoldering green eyes.

"I guess we do."

He walked over and kissed me before leading me to the couch. Once he was seated, I dropped to my knees between his outstretched legs.

I was just getting into sucking Ryan off when I heard something slam into the wall, and I immediately sat back and looked toward the sound.

"Fuck!" Sean yelled as he rubbed his hip, and the console table next to him wobbled.

"Holy shit!" Ryan shouted. "Aren't you supposed to still be at work?"

My boss kept his back to us and replied, "I came straight home after court instead of going to the office."

"Sean, I'm so sorry," I said as Ryan pulled up his pants.

I was beyond humiliated and wondered if Sean was going to fire me on the spot.

"You can turn around now," Ryan told his father as soon as he zipped up.

Sean spun around slowly, and I turned my gaze to the floor, unable to look at him. "That was completely unprofessional. I should go."

"Can't say I was expecting to walk in on that, but you don't have to rush out of here."

"I already finished cooking. I'll make your plate and then be on my way." I hurried off to the kitchen.

Ryan joined me a few seconds later as I put the salmon back in the oven to warm it up. "You good?"

I shook my head. "Your dad is going to fire me."

"No, he isn't."

"How can you be sure? He just caught me giving you a blow job on his couch."

"Yeah, but we're both consenting adults. If anything, he's madder at me. He's seen the way I flirt with you. Besides he'd hate to lose you as a chef."

We continued to chat as I heated up dinner and worried about my job. Eventually Sean walked into the kitchen, putting an end to my conversation with Ryan.

I opened the oven to get Sean's food and then plated the fish, brown rice, and asparagus. "I made salmon tonight." While continuing to avoid eye contact, I placed it in front of him, then grabbed some silverware and a napkin and set them beside his plate. "Would you like some wine as well?"

"That would be great," he replied.

I uncorked a bottle of pinot noir and filled a glass.

"You're not eating?" Sean asked Ryan.

"I had a late lunch with a client, so I'm not hungry, but I will take a glass of wine."

The room went silent as I poured Ryan a glass, and Sean began eating. After a few minutes, I broke the awkward quietness. "I'm going to head out. All of your meals for the weekend are in the fridge."

"Thank you." Sean wiped his mouth with his napkin. "I'll see you on Monday if I get home before you finish up."

Relief washed over me as I realized I hadn't lost my job. "Sounds good."

THE HOLIDAY RUSH MADE THE NEXT COUPLE OF MONTHS FLY BY. It seemed as though I was cooking for multiple parties every week during December, but things seemed to settle down once we got past the new year.

As I made my way to Sean's place, I popped in my ear buds and listened to Surrender's new album, "Neon Nights." It became an immediate success when it was released a couple of weeks prior, and even though hearing Malachi's voice reminded me of the few months I got to be with him, those bittersweet feelings didn't stop me from playing it on repeat.

When I got to my boss's condo, I pulled out the ingredients to make a beef Wellington for his monthly family dinner. Shortly after I got started on the meal, Ryan arrived and sat at the island across from me. The two of us still hooked up on occasion, but we no longer messed around at his father's place.

As I wrapped the prepared beef tenderloin in puff pastry, I heard the front door open. Even though Ryan and I weren't doing anything, I still felt a twinge of embarrassment remembering when Sean had walked in on us. It had taken weeks before I could look him in the eye again.

Morgan, Sean's daughter, walked around the corner and smirked when she saw Ryan was already there. "Should I leave so you guys can be alone, or did you already finish?"

I groaned while Ryan barked out a laugh. When I'd learned he had told Morgan what happened, I had been mortified, but he promised it wasn't a big deal. Since then, it had been a running joke between the three of us.

"Just finished," Ryan teased.

"Eww. It was funny when I said it. Not so much when you admit to it," she huffed and took a seat next to her brother.

"Don't worry. Nothing happened." I glared at Ryan.

"Not yet, at least." He winked.

I wasn't opposed to what he was suggesting. The thing I had with Ryan worked because neither of us was looking for anything serious, so we got together whenever it was convenient. Since I'd fallen hard—much harder than I'd expected—for Malachi, and it had hurt like hell when he left, I was wary of getting into a committed relationship again. Since then, I'd used casual hook ups to try to forget about the man I could never have. Much to my dismay, it hadn't worked, and when I was alone at night, with my hand wrapped around my cock, it was only Malachi I thought of.

As they continued to chat, I started boiling potatoes.

"So, I've been listening to Surrender's new album non-stop. It's amazing, and I heard they are going on tour in a couple of months," Morgan said out of nowhere, and immediately my ears perked up.

I received regular updates from my brother about what the band was doing and saw a lot of posts on social media about them, but I hadn't talked to Malachi since the night they'd won *The Band Showdown*. Even when the guys were on the East Coast for the holidays, I avoided him, telling my brother I had catering gigs every day except Christmas when Malachi was with his family.

From what I could tell, Malachi had moved on and was fully embracing the rock star lifestyle. Pictures of him were plastered everywhere on social media, and he had a different woman on his arm in almost every photo. And while I wanted only good things for him, I didn't think I could handle seeing him in person again. It would hurt too much because I still missed what we once had.

"We should go to one of their concerts," Ryan stated.

"Duh. Of course, I'm going, but I was wondering if Jasper here could hook me up," Morgan said.

Morgan was what could be described as a Surrender superfan. When she had found out I grew up in Southborough and my last name was Bennett, she'd asked if I was related to Jesse. She could hardly contain her excitement when I told her he was my brother.

"Can't you just use Dad's credit card to buy a ticket like you do for everything else?" Ryan asked his sister.

She rolled her eyes. "I'm going to buy my own ticket, asshole." She turned to me, her voice taking on a much sweeter tone. "But I thought maybe you could get me backstage?"

"Uh, I don't know how that all works, but I can ask my brother the next time I talk to him."

"You're the best." She jumped up and hugged me.

I glanced at Ryan, my eyes wide.

He laughed. "You just made her day. She has the biggest crush on Malachi Danvers."

Who didn't?

10

MALACHI

I sat at the long conference table in our manager's office, tapping my fingers lightly on the polished wood. The afternoon sun streaming through the tall windows cast a golden hue on the band posters that adorned the walls and made the room warm.

My bandmates, Savannah, and the guys from Midnight Thunder, the band opening for us, were seated around me, each absorbed in their own thoughts. I hadn't seen Savannah since we'd hooked up after recording "Whispers in the Night." We both knew it was a one-night thing. Hell, maybe it would turn into more than a one off since she was going on tour with us. I wasn't looking for a relationship, but if she was down to fuck, I wasn't going to turn her away.

At the end of the table, Rina, our manager, sat with her laptop open and a stack of papers beside her. She clapped her hands together to gather everyone's attention. "All right, let's get started. We need to finalize the setlist for the tour and discuss logistics and some other things."

"Let's start with the setlist," I suggested. "We need to make sure it flows well and keeps the energy up."

Jesse looked up from his phone. "I was thinking we should open with 'Rising Tide.' It's a strong start and gets the crowd pumped from the get-go."

Elliott nodded. "Yeah, and we can follow it up with 'Echoes of Tomorrow.' That bass line is killer and transitions perfectly."

I scribbled notes on my notepad as we continued to put our set together. "How about 'Midnight Reverie' in the middle? It's slower, but it showcases our range."

Silas stopped tapping his sticks, his brow furrowed in thought. "I like that. And then we can bring the energy back up with 'Fading Lights,' 'Crimson Sky,' 'Chasing Shadows,' 'Gravity Pull,', and 'Silver Lining' before we hit the finale with Savannah."

Rina's fingers flew over the keyboard as she made notes on her laptop. "Great suggestions. Remember, we also need to consider the timing and any potential encores."

I exchanged a glance with Jesse, who gave a subtle nod.

"We should definitely save 'Surrender' for the encore," I said. "It's our namesake and the perfect closing song."

She smiled approvingly. "Sounds like we have a solid setlist. Now, about the tour logistics. We'll start in Toronto and then hit major cities across Canada and the US."

"We need to make sure our gear gets to every show on time. Last time we were in Canada, we had a mix-up with customs. It was a nightmare," Jesse stated.

Rina nodded. "I remember, and I've already arranged for a more reliable transportation service. Everything will be where it needs to be, I promise."

Silas looked up. "Any press interviews?"

Rina nodded. "A few, but I've kept the schedule light so you all have time to rest and prepare between shows."

I caught her eye and gave her a grateful smile. "Thanks. You're making this easy for us."

She waved off the thanks, but her eyes softened. "Just doing my job. Now, any other concerns or suggestions before we get into some other things?"

"I know I'm new and all and kinda like tagging along, but any chance we can get vegan options for me?" Savannah asked. "It's not always easy to find places to eat on the road."

"I'm glad you brought up food," Rina said. "That brings us to a minor issue."

"An issue? What kind of issue?" Jesse pressed.

"Our caterers fell through yesterday, and we need to find someone fast," Rina replied.

"How about my brother?" Jesse questioned.

I sucked in a small breath. "Jasper?"

"Yeah." Jesse nodded as if he had more than one brother. "I bet he'd be stoked to do it."

"He's back in the States?" I asked. Last I'd heard, he had stayed in Paris after he finished culinary school.

"Has been for a while," Jesse answered.

My mind was racing at the thought of Jasper going on tour with us. The mention of him brought back all the memories of what we once had. Every secret kiss, every time I snuck through his window. The way he tasted, smelled, and felt in my arms.

Jesse and Rina discussed more about him, but I was lost in my thoughts, imagining his smile, his voice, just him in my life once more. The possibility of being close to him again was making my heart race. I missed him more than I wanted to admit, even to myself. What if he didn't feel the same about me? What if he was seeing someone?

Glancing down at the crescent moon on my wrist, I wondered if he still had his. I'd gotten a few more tats over the years, but I never added to the moon or covered it up. Did he?

"Let me call him," Jesse said, bringing me out of my thoughts.

"Great." Rina stood. "Let's take a break while you make the call."

What if Jasper said yes?

It still hurt to think about the last time I'd gotten to see him ...

The car Stellar Records, Surrender's new record label, ordered for me and Jesse, arrived at the bistro where we were meeting our fami-

lies. He and I slid out of the car and walked inside the restaurant. Immediately, I spotted my sister as she waved her hand in the air and flagged us over to where they were seated at a large table for all of us.

"There they are!" Mom beamed as she stood and rushed to hug me.

Everyone was still on a high from winning The Band Showdown. Who was I kidding? I was fucking ecstatic too. Jesse and I had just come from a photoshoot for Celebrity Style and in the morning, we were appearing on Sunrise LA to talk about being the winners and what was to come next. That, of course, was to record our first album.

"Are you guys wearing makeup?" Norah asked as she hugged me.

"Don't be jealous, we just worked it for the cameras," I teased.

"I'm totally jealous, but happy for you."

"Thanks, sis."

"We all are happy for you two," Mr. B stated. "Silas and Elliott too."

Our other bandmates were meeting with their families at other places before everyone returned to Boston. The guys and I were staying in LA while we finished up everything that came with winning the reality competition.

I was torn with how to feel because a part of me wanted to go home and see if Jasper and I could pick up where we left off, but the other part of me knew Surrender was finally going to live the dream. Somehow Jesse and Olivia were going to make it work, so maybe Jasper and I could too?

After the hugs with everyone were out of the way, I took a seat across from Jasper, realizing he hadn't hugged me. "You okay?" I asked him.

He swallowed. "Yeah. Just a lot on my mind."

"He's flying to Paris in a few hours," his mom cut in.

I balked. "Paris?"

"I'm starting culinary school there next week," Jasper said.

Before I could ask him more, the waiter approached and took everyone's order. Nothing more was said about Paris or the fact that *even if the guys and I returned to Boston, Jasper wouldn't be there, and the reality hit me hard.*

I suppose in the back of my mind, I always assumed Jasper would be there waiting for me when I returned home. But as I looked at him, I felt a pang of something deeper. It wasn't just the loss of a friend or the distance that was about to stretch between us—it was the realization of how much he meant to me.

His eyes met mine, and I wanted to tell him. To reach across the table, take his hand, and spill everything I was thinking. The truth was, I was in love with him. I had been for a long time, even before we started secretly dating.

But I couldn't. Not now. Not when he was about to live his own dream.

I forced a smile, nodding in understanding as our families chatted around us. During the meal, I watched as he laughed with everyone as if nothing had changed.

But I finally realized it had.

11

Jasper

My phone rang as I sat at the dining table in the apartment I shared with another chef. Garrett and I met when we worked at the same restaurant after I returned from France. We had quickly formed a friendship and decided to be roommates.

Glancing at my phone, I saw my brother's name on the screen, and I smiled as I answered. "Hey, bro. What's up?"

"Hey, I'm glad I actually caught you. Gotta a minute to talk, or are you working?"

Jesse and I texted each other about once a week, but with our busy schedules, we didn't get many opportunities to chat.

"Just writing up a grocery list. What's up?"

"The guys and I are meeting with our manager about our upcoming tour."

I put my pen down. "Okay …"

I had no idea why he was calling me about his band stuff, but if he was talking about his upcoming concerts, maybe I would get a chance to ask him about backstage passes for Ryan and Morgan.

"Turns out the company they were going to use for catering fell through. I suggested they hire you, and our manager agreed to offer you the job if you want it."

"For real?"

"Yeah. Say you'll do it."

"I don't know. I have clients who depend on me."

"I know, but think of all the doors this could open for you. The record label would be a great connection for you later."

He had a good point. "What all does the job entail? Would I be cooking for hundreds of people every day?"

He chuckled. "It's nice you think we're so big we'll have hundreds with us on this tour, but no. I don't know all the details yet, but you'll probably only have to do a big dinner on show nights. Otherwise, it's just us, our manager, a couple of directors, Midnight Thunder who will be opening for us, and Savannah Sky. You know the guys and I are chill about what we eat, but you'll need to make some vegan options for Savannah and maybe some other staffers."

"Savannah Sky is going on tour with you?"

"Did I not mention it when we last talked?"

"Uh, no." I snorted. "Pretty sure I would have remembered if you had." Savannah Sky was an up-and-coming pop star with incredible vocal range who had recorded a song with Malachi. Between her blonde bombshell looks and being featured on Surrender's new album, she had become a regular on all the celebrity gossip sites.

"Yeah, it seems everyone loves 'Whispers in the Night,' so as long as Malachi can keep his dick in his pants and not make her mad, she'll be performing it with us. There's going to be an announcement about it tomorrow."

My stomach dropped at the mention of Malachi being with someone else. "What do you mean? Are they together?"

Jesse laughed. "No, but I'm pretty sure she has a thing for him. You know how he is, though. No serious relationships for him."

"Dude, fuck off," Malachi grumbled in the background and hearing his voice again made my heart race.

"Anyway, what do you think about the job? You'll get to travel all around the US and Canada. I know how much you love visiting new places."

It was true. After I finished culinary school in Paris, I took advantage of the train system in Europe and visited several other countries. My goal was to one day travel across the US since I had seen little outside of the Northeast.

"It's a lot to think about," I said. "When do you need an answer?"

"Like in a week. Rina suggested you come out next month and start cooking for us during rehearsals. It will give you a few weeks to figure out anything you might need and work with the label to get it all set up. She also said it would be a good idea for you to bring an assistant if you know of anyone."

"Okay, I'll let you know."

I SPENT THE NEXT FEW DAYS WEIGHING THE PROS AND CONS OF GOING on tour with Surrender. Jesse was right about one thing; working for a major record label had the potential to boost my career. Plus, traveling and spending time with my brother would be great. But one thing held me back—or rather, one person.

Malachi Danvers.

Being in his presence every single day had the potential to make me fall for him all over again, and I didn't know if I could handle having my heart broken for a second time.

I shook my head, trying to rid it of the intrusive thoughts. Malachi wasn't out as being bi. I didn't know if he ever would be, and for that reason along with him being Jesse's best friend, I knew nothing could ever happen openly between us.

I entered my apartment and saw my roommate, Garrett, standing at the stove.

"Hey, what's up?" he asked when he noticed me.

"Not much. You got work tonight?"

He shrugged. "I do, but I'm not looking forward to it. Nigel has been a terror lately, and I'm sure he's going to yell at me the whole time I'm there."

Nigel, the head chef at the restaurant where I used to work with Garrett, was a dick. It wasn't unheard of in the restaurant industry, but I understood why Garrett wasn't looking forward to his shift.

I took a seat at the dining table, which sat just off the entrance to the kitchen. "About that. I've got something I wanted to run by you."

He turned off the burner and spun around. "Yeah?"

I nodded. "My brother offered me a job as the chef on his upcoming tour."

"Seriously? That's awesome. Are you going to do it?"

Despite my concern about being around Malachi, the more I thought about it, I couldn't deny how great of an opportunity it was. And maybe seeing Malachi wouldn't be that big of a deal. Years had passed since we were together. Time had a way of changing people, and it was possible I was worried about nothing. Surely the feelings I had before wouldn't be the same now. At least, I could hope that was the case.

"I think so, and when I was talking to Jesse, he mentioned I should find another chef to help me out. You interested?"

Garrett's eyes lit up. "You want me to work with you?"

"Of course. We already know we make a great team in the kitchen, and I know you're dying to tell Nigel to shove it. We're on a month-to-month lease here. Seems like perfect timing to me."

"Hell yeah." He walked over and pulled me up into a bro hug. "Let's do this."

"Cool. I'll let my brother know, and then we can work out the details once I have more information."

I headed toward my room and called Jesse. It rang a few times and then went to voicemail. Instead of leaving a message, I sent him a text:

> I'm in

A few minutes later, my phone buzzed.

> Jesse: Awesome! Can't wait to see you

ONCE I DECIDED TO TAKE THE JOB, I HAD TO LET ALL MY CLIENTS know. I walked to Sean Ashford's door and entered the code on the keypad to let myself in. I had texted him earlier to see what time he'd be home and told him I had something to discuss with him.

While working on dinner, I heard the door open, followed by two familiar voices. Ryan was with his father, and I was both grateful I could talk to them together and a little bummed my new job meant saying goodbye to Ryan as well.

It wasn't because I wanted something more with him than the casual thing we had going, but I considered him a friend, and I enjoyed hanging out with him.

"Hey, Jasper," Sean greeted. "I'm going to put my stuff down, and then I'll be back."

"Okay. Dinner should be ready in about thirty minutes." I smiled.

When Sean walked away, Ryan sat at the island where he usually watched me cook. "Dad said you had something to talk to him about."

I nodded, but said nothing.

"Is everything all right?"

"Yeah, just work stuff."

"Ah. Gotcha. Maybe we can hit up Chrome after you're done here," he suggested.

Any other night, I would have jumped at the chance to grab a couple of drinks and dance, but I had a lot I needed to do prior to leaving for LA.

"I wish I could, but tonight won't work."

He looked a little disappointed. "Raincheck, then?"

Before I could commit to going out another night, Sean returned and poured himself a glass of Macallan.

"Either of you want one?" He lifted the bottle.

Some people may have found it strange he would offer me a drink when I was there to prepare meals for him, but Sean never treated me as though I was just an employee. It set him apart from most of my other clients and was one of the reasons I would miss working for him the most.

"I'm good, but thank you," I replied.

"You know I'll never pass up a glass of your favorite whisky." Ryan chuckled.

Once they both had their drinks, Sean took a seat and addressed me, "So you had something you wanted to discuss?"

"I do." I turned on the oven so it could preheat and then took a deep breath and faced him. "I'm putting in my two weeks' notice."

Sean's and Ryan's eyes went wide, and then Sean spoke. "Oh. I wasn't expecting that."

"I'm sorry. I've really enjoyed working for you, but my brother offered me a job while he's on tour, and it's too good of an opportunity to pass up."

"Wait," Ryan said. "Are you telling us you're going on tour with Surrender?"

I nodded. "Yeah."

"Holy shit. Wait until I tell Morgan. You know she's going to be bugging your ass even more for those backstage passes now."

I laughed. "I still don't know how that all works, but I'll do my best to hook you guys up with something when the tour comes here." My eyes flicked back to Sean. "I hope you can understand my decision."

He stood and walked around the island to shake my hand. "Of course I do. Not many people get a chance to travel around the country with a famous rock band, and it would be silly not to do it."

"Thank you."

He patted my shoulder. "And if you find yourself back in Boston and need a job, give me a call."

"I appreciate it."

The next two weeks were jam-packed, and before I knew it, I was in LA. Olivia picked me up from the airport, and we stopped by her and Jesse's house to drop off my luggage before driving me to the warehouse where Surrender was rehearsing so I could meet up with everyone. Garrett was going to join us in Toronto when the tour started because he still had some shit to wrap up back home, so I was all by myself.

We checked in with a security guard at the gate, and then she stopped next to the building. "I've got an appointment to get to, but I'll see you later tonight. We're really happy you're here."

I leaned over and gave her a quick hug. "Thanks."

Grabbing my notebook so I could take notes of everyone's dietary preferences, I slid out of the car and gave her a little wave before she drove away. Turning around, I took a deep breath. The only thing standing between me and seeing Malachi again was the large steel door in front of me. Gathering all the courage I could muster, I pulled it open.

Malachi's deep, smooth voice filled my ears as I stepped inside. The band was up on the makeshift stage, the bright lights shining down on them. It was dark where I stood, so I didn't think they could see me from where they practiced.

He looked different from the guy I remembered. His dark brown hair was longer and hung over his forehead, almost covering his striking green eyes. He'd also bulked up, making the sleeves of his black T-shirt look as though they barely fit over his biceps, which flexed as he gripped the microphone. The years had been extremely kind to him, and I knew I was screwed. There was no way I could look at him every day and not want to relive all the secret moments we'd once shared.

As I walked closer, I could see he had more tattoos than the last time I saw him, but the crescent moon on his wrist that matched mine had been left untouched. It surprised me he hadn't covered it up.

12

MALACHI

Grabbing a bottle of water, I downed the entire thing in one huge gulp. We'd been rehearsing for over two hours, and while we knew our setlist forward and backward, it was still tiring. Hell, preparing to go on tour was exhausting, but it was what we'd always wanted.

As I wiped the sweat from my brow, I saw someone watching us from the back of the warehouse. My heart skipped a beat, knowing exactly who it was.

Jasper.

He looked almost the same, maybe a bit more refined or taller. His dirty blond hair was short and spiked slightly in the front, and unlike when he was in high school, he sported a hint of stubble on his face that only added to how hot he was. *Fuck.* Seeing him brought a flood of memories—late nights sneaking around, secret kisses, and how it all ended abruptly so I could live my dream.

"Jasper!" Jesse called as soon as he saw him. "You made it."

Jasper walked closer, and Jesse hopped off the stage to hug his brother. I felt the urge to do the same, but didn't. How weird would that be? Would it be weird? It wasn't as though we'd been in contact the last three and a half years, but I suddenly wanted to feel him in my arms again. Elliott and Silas jumped down too, and greeted Jasper with bro hugs. Maybe it wouldn't be weird to hug him, but before I could think more about it, Jesse noticed me staring and waved me over.

I forced a smile as I joined them. "Hey, Jasper."

"Malachi," he replied with a nod, and then we each took a hesitant step forward and hugged. "Good to see you."

"Yeah, you too." I stepped back as though that simple contact would trigger alarm bells, and everyone would know our long-held secret. To avoid any questions, I turned to Savannah, who was standing nearby. "Savannah, this is Jasper, Jesse's brother."

She extended her hand. "Nice to meet you, Jasper. I've heard great things about your food."

"Thanks." He grinned, shaking her hand. "I'm looking forward to cooking for all of you."

"We've got about another hour of rehearsal, and then maybe all of us can go grab a drink?" Jesse suggested, then playfully punched Jasper on the shoulder. "Celebrate you finally being a part of Surrender."

"Sounds good to me." Jasper flicked his gaze to me briefly. "Maybe before we go, I can get everyone's food preferences so I can start planning some menus."

"Yeah, we can do that. Just hang out for a bit. There are snacks and drinks over there." Jesse pointed in the direction of the table with various platters from Costco since the caterer fell through and we were waiting for Jasper to arrive.

"All right." Jasper nodded.

Everyone left, and I stood awkwardly until Jasper said, "Guess we'll be seeing a lot of each other."

"Yeah, looks like it." I was unsure of what else to say.

Just like old times. No, I can't say that.

Before the silence could last long, Savannah yelled from the stage, "Malachi, we're ready for our duet!"

I gave Jasper another small, tight smile. "Duty calls. It was good to see you."

"You too."

I turned and jogged back to the stage.

"Ready?" Savannah asked as she stood at her mic.

"Always." I took my place beside her.

The music started, and we began to sing. As our voices intertwined, I couldn't help but feel the chemistry between us that had ignited when we'd first recorded "Whispers in the Night." Her hand brushed against mine, and she winked. I leaned in, playing up the song as though we were lovers and our voices rose and fell together in perfect harmony.

Between verses, I caught Jasper watching us, but I didn't let it distract me. Instead, I focused on Savannah and pretended every word was about her when, really, it was about the man who was now only a few feet away and not several thousands of miles like he used to be.

> *"My thoughts of you begin to race*
> *Especially when I see your face in every embrace*
> *Every heartbeat, every tear, I keep holding on, wishing*
> *you were near*
> *Longing for the moment when you'll be here"*

As the last notes were sung, Savannah laughed softly, leaning closer. "I still can't get over how amazing you are," she whispered, her breath tickling my ear. "And I'm not just talking about singing."

"You're not so bad yourself," I replied, our eyes locking for a moment longer than necessary.

"Maybe after drinks with the band, we can pick up from our night together?"

Immediately, I looked around, and my gaze collided with Jasper's. It wasn't as though we were anything to each other anymore, but flirting with her and having her ask to hook up while he was nearby felt weird. Felt wrong. However, I still said, "Maybe."

Rina ordered two vehicles to take us to get drinks after we finished with rehearsal. The SUV rolled to a stop in front of The Velvet Veil, a nightclub in West Hollywood. I could already see the flashing lights from the paparazzi, their cameras ready to capture every move we made. I took a deep breath to brace myself for the chaos. No matter how much I loved the rock star life, being followed by paps and having almost every move I made documented fucking sucked.

After opening the door of the Suburban, I stepped out and extended a hand to Savannah. The crowd of photographers surged forward, shouting our names and snapping photos. Her hand slipped into mine, and her golden hair caught the camera flashes as she emerged from the SUV. For a brief second, our fingers laced together. I glanced over at the other vehicle just as Jasper stepped out with Jesse and Silas. Jasper's eyes locked onto our joined hands, and I dropped Savannah's hand as if it were on fire. The cameras continued to click, questions being thrown out about the album and upcoming tour, but we ignored them.

"Ready to have some fun?" Savannah asked, looping her arm through mine as Elliott closed the door behind us.

"Absolutely," I replied. I was ready to have a few drinks in hopes that would somehow make me more comfortable with Jasper around. It was weird, not only because we had our secret from the past, but I also felt as though I was cheating on him in a way. Maybe that was because seeing him again made me feel as though I still had feelings for him. Did I?

Our group walked inside, while the paparazzi faded behind us. The club was dimly lit, with music blaring and people dancing. Some turned and looked at us as Jesse led our group to the VIP section, where a reserved table awaited with a bottle of vodka in an ice bucket.

Jesse poured us all shots and then raised his glass and said, "To having Jasper with us on tour."

"To Jasper," we echoed, our glasses clinking together. I downed the shot and my eyes involuntarily drifted to Jasper. He was looking at me too, and we exchanged small smiles. What was he thinking? Did he find it weird that we were acting like there had been nothing between us before? It wasn't as though we were about to tell everyone, but the entire thing was awkward. Would this be how the entire tour would go?

"Thanks for having me," Jasper said sincerely, his gaze fixed on me. "I'm excited to be with you guys again."

Savannah leaned into me, her hand brushing against my arm. "So, what's the plan for tonight?" she asked, her voice low and flirtatious.

"Celebrating Jasper, right?" I replied, forcing a smile.

"Yeah, but after we leave?" She winked.

"We'll just have to see."

A cocktail waitress came over and we each ordered drinks or what we wanted to mix the vodka with. The alcohol flowed as the night wore on, except I stuck to only two, because even though it was assumed I lived the rock star lifestyle, I was still well aware about my family's history with addiction, mainly my grandfather.

At one point, Jesse left to call Olivia. Elliott was on the dance floor with Savannah, and Silas was in the bathroom, where he frequently ran off to any time we went out. It was just me and Jasper alone.

"It's been a while," Jasper said quietly, his eyes searching mine.

"Yeah, it has," I agreed. "How've you been?"

"Busy. I've been working as a private chef and my clients keep me on my toes. But it's good. I've missed this, though. Being around you guys."

"We've missed you too," I said softly, wanting to elaborate and tell him *I* missed him the most. I caught a glimpse of the crescent moon tattoo on his wrist and smiled as I realized he hadn't covered it up.

"Look—" Jasper started, but Savannah returned.

She slid into her seat beside me and rested her hand on my leg. "I'm ready to get out of here if you are."

"I'm going to go get another drink," Jasper muttered as he slipped out of the booth.

"Wait." I reached for him.

"It's cool. We'll catch up another time."

"Sorry, did I interrupt something?" Savannah asked as Jasper walked away.

I swallowed. "Just trying to catch up."

"Well, I meant what I said. I'm ready to get out of here."

No matter how much I wanted to get off, Savannah wasn't the one I wanted to be with.

"Not tonight. I'm tired."

She blinked. "Tired?"

"You've only been here today to rehearse our duet. We've been putting in long hours to get ready for the tour."

She leaned in closer and said into my ear, "I'm really fucking horny, Malachi. Let's get off together and then you can crash."

I was about to tell her no again, but Elliott joined us. "There you are, Savvy. You ditched me."

I blinked as he called her by a nickname, not realizing they were so close but that gave me an idea. "She's ready to go. Can you ride with her to make sure she gets home safely?"

Elliott blinked. "You're sure?"

I gave him a look that I hoped he took to mean I didn't care if they hooked up. "If she wants. I'm going to head home myself."

"Alone?" he asked.

"Yeah, alone?" Savannah questioned.

"Sorry, Savvy. I'm beat."

She slid out of the seat and grabbed Elliott's hand. "Your loss, Malachi."

My eyes moved to where Jasper was leaning on the bar, his back to us. "El will take good care of you."

THE FOLLOWING DAY, I WOKE TO MY CELL RINGING FAR TOO EARLY. I grabbed it and squinted as the bright glow hurt my eyes and saw that it was Rina calling me.

"Hey, what's up?"

"Tell me you've seen it."

"Seen what?"

"The picture of you and Savannah Sky holding hands last night."

"No." I rolled onto my back. "I was sleeping."

Once Savannah and Elliott had left, Silas returned from the bathroom, and then Jesse came back to say Olivia was waiting for him. It was the same song and dance. Jasper left too since was staying with Jesse until we went on tour, so we all parted ways.

When I'd gotten back to my condo, I couldn't stop thinking about Jasper. I lay in my bed, and the memories returned. They quickly drifted to our times together in his bed when I would sneak in through his window, and before I knew it, I was jerking off as I remembered how good his hand felt around my dick, how he knew how hard to fist me and how fast to pump my stiff cock.

Once I was spent, I cleaned up and crashed. I had no clue about pictures of me and Savannah, though I didn't care. I was used to the media speculating if I had something more than casual going on with anyone I was seen with.

"Well, it's all over *Star Nation*, and there's speculation that maybe you're dating."

I rolled my eyes. "Okay?"

"And Stellar Records wants you to go with it."

I sat up. "Go with what?"

"Pretend you're dating while on tour."

13

Jasper

Jesse and I walked through the parking lot toward the warehouse where I'd met up with the guys the day before. While my brother and his bandmates did the rehearsal thing, I was supposed to meet with Ken, a guy from purchasing at Stellar Records, to go over everything the label needed to purchase or rent for me for the tour.

When I first arrived, I was slightly worried about the logistics of cooking on the road, but my concerns were quickly alleviated when I learned I wasn't expected to prepare three gourmet meals every single day. When we were in the cities where Surrender was performing, we would all stay at a hotel, and everyone would likely eat there or at local restaurants. I would cook lunch and dinner on concert days for the guys, Savannah, Midnight Thunder, and the crew traveling with us, as well as make simple things that could be heated up in the buses as we drove to the next location. And while it sounded as though it would be a relatively easy gig, I still needed some special equipment since I didn't have a full-size kitchen to operate out of.

As we entered the building, my gaze immediately moved to where

Malachi and Savannah sat on the edge of the stage. It felt as though I was on high alert whenever we were near each other, and I couldn't stop myself from seeking him out. He was speaking to Rina while Savannah pressed against his side, gazing at him with stars in her eyes. It was much the same way she had looked at him at the club, and I couldn't stop the wave of jealousy that washed over me every time I saw them together.

Turning away from the cozy scene, I followed my brother to the coffee station where Silas and Elliott stood.

"Good morning," Silas grumbled as we approached, and I wondered how he was going to get through practice with what appeared to be a massive hangover.

"Morning. What's going on over there?" Jesse lifted his head toward Malachi.

"You didn't hear?" Elliott asked. "The gossip sites are reporting that those two are in a relationship, and now the label wants them to fake it. Stellar Records thinks it'll be good for publicity."

I'd heard about film studios doing something similar with their lead actors when a movie came out, but I always thought it was just a rumor. Apparently, it happened in the music industry as well.

"So, they aren't actually dating?" I asked.

At the club, when Savannah had asked Malachi to leave with her, I was convinced there was something going on between them, but then he'd asked Elliott to make sure she got home okay. The entire situation was confusing, but I was desperate to know if she and Malachi were together.

Jesse shook his head. "Nope."

"They hooked up once, but that was it," Elliott added.

"Why do I have a feeling this is going to backfire?" Jesse sighed. "He knows nothing about being in a relationship."

My brother may have never seen it, but I knew he was wrong. Immediately, I thought back to all the times Malachi had showed me he cared, like when I had been stung by a bee and he'd refused to leave my side and kept me calm. Or when he had suggested we get matching tattoos because I was nervous about getting my first one. Based on my experience, I had no doubt in my mind he could play the doting boyfriend if he wanted to.

While the guys continued to chat about how much of a bad idea the record label's plan was, I couldn't keep from glancing at Malachi. Even though I knew what was going on, I wondered if Savannah was playing along because she had been asked to or because she hoped it would turn into the real thing. Having witnessed her flirting with him the night before, I wouldn't have been surprised if she wanted more, and who could blame her?

THE REST OF MY TIME IN LA FLEW BY AS WE MADE THE FINAL preparations for the tour, and in less than an hour, I was going to board a flight to Toronto with everyone for their first show.

Between the long, exhausting rehearsal hours, and taking care of shit in their personal lives before they hit the road for several months, everyone usually went their separate ways as soon as they were done practicing. And since I was crashing at Jesse's place and didn't have my own vehicle, I had no choice but to go with him. On the occasion we did all hang out, Malachi and I never got the opportunity to have a private conversation.

I tried to convince myself I was fine with it. He didn't owe me anything, and I knew his focus was on his career, but that didn't stop me from wishing we could have a few minutes alone. A part of me wanted, or rather, needed to know if there was still something between us or if my feelings were one-sided, but it was impossible to figure it out with people around us all the time.

I found a seat at the gate with the other crew members while Rina tried to usher the guys, Savannah, and Olivia, who was traveling with the band, off to the first-class lounge.

"Maybe I should try to upgrade your ticket," Jesse said. "That way, you can stay with us."

I shook my head, not wanting to accept his offer since everyone other than the band was flying coach and I didn't want to appear as though I was getting special treatment. "I'm good. Besides, I have some planning to do that will keep me busy during the flight."

Jesse nodded. "Okay. See you on the plane."

As they all walked away, my gaze honed in on Malachi's perfect ass. I was so focused on checking him out, it took a second before I noticed him glance over his shoulder. When our eyes met, he raised an eyebrow and smirked.

Busted.

> Jesse: We're going down to the bar for drinks. You and Garrett should come meet us

WE HAD ARRIVED AT THE HOTEL TWO HOURS AGO, AND GARRETT WAS already sawing logs.

> Me: He's asleep but I'll head down in a minute

I grabbed my wallet and key and slipped out of the room, making sure not to wake my friend. As I entered the hotel bar, I spotted Jesse waving me over to their table in the corner. The only open seat was next to Malachi, so with no other option, I pulled out the chair and sat down. A server quickly came over and, after he took my drink order, I asked the guys, "You all ready for your first show tomorrow?"

Malachi grinned and took a drink of his rum and Coke. "For sure. Getting to headline our own tour has always been the dream. Sometimes I still can't believe we get to do this for a living."

"It's fucking awesome." Jesse wrapped his arm around his girlfriend's shoulders. "I'm just glad I get to share it with all of you and my favorite girl."

Olivia gave him a quick peck. "I wouldn't miss it for the world."

The two of them had been together for years, and it was clear how in love with each other they still were after all this time.

"You two are adorable," Savannah cooed, and Olivia smiled.

"I'll be right back," Silas said as he pushed away from the table and stood.

The guys silently watched as he made his way toward the bathroom. Once the door closed behind him, Elliott addressed the table. "We need to keep an eye on him."

Malachi nodded. "He said he had everything under control, but I'm not so sure."

The server returned with my vodka soda, and I took a sip. "What's going on with Silas?"

I wasn't sure it was my place to ask, but he'd been best friends with my brother for years, and now I considered all of them friends of mine too.

Jesse exchanged a look with Elliott and Malachi before he turned to me. "You know we all like to have a good time and party, but Silas has sort of taken that to the extreme lately. We're just a little worried about him."

I remembered Silas used to hang out with Donnie Pierce who supplied a lot of the kids at our high school with weed, but I didn't think he'd ever done more than smoke a little pot. Maybe things had changed. "Have you talked to him about it?"

Elliott nodded. "He brushed it off, but did say he'd stay drug free during the tour."

"We're a family," Malachi added. "We'll watch out for him."

His words served as another reminder of why a relationship between us was forbidden. He saw my brother as family, and that was important to Malachi.

A few minutes later, Silas returned, and I found myself looking for any signs he had been doing drugs in the bathroom. It wasn't because I was judging him, but I was concerned now that I was aware of what was going on. Still, I saw no evidence he'd done anything. He was alert but chill and able to carry on a coherent conversation with the rest of us.

"So, what's your plan for tomorrow?" Jesse asked me as I swallowed another drink of my cocktail.

"Garrett and I need to go shopping for groceries in the morning, and then I guess I'll spend the rest of the day getting used to cooking in a mobile kitchen."

"You always did a good job when we went camping. I'm sure this will be easy compared to that," Malachi stated.

His compliment hit me right in the feels, and a memory of our first kiss in the tent flashed through my mind. "Yeah, but you and Jesse eat pretty much anything. I've got more people to please now."

"Just promise me you're not going to make us all eat vegan shit because of Savannah," Elliott teased.

"What's wrong with vegan meals?" Savannah stuck out her tongue at Elliott and he winked.

"Nothing." I grinned in Savannah's direction. "I've got some damn good recipes I plan on making."

She peered around Malachi and smiled at me. "Thanks, Jasper. I really appreciate it."

As much as I hated the idea of her fake dating Malachi, I'd gotten to know her a little bit over the past couple of weeks and her sweet personality made it impossible not to like her.

"Not a problem at all."

We ordered another round of drinks, paid the tab, and then Jesse and Olivia were the first to head back to their room. It didn't take long for Elliott and Silas to follow, leaving me alone with Malachi and Savannah. I was just about to excuse myself when Savannah's phone buzzed on the table.

"Oh, that's my agent. We're in negotiations for some sponsorships, so I'm going to call it a night."

As she stood to leave, the unmistakable flash of a camera lit up the space. Her eyes went wide, and then, as if she remembered she was supposed to be dating Malachi, she bent down and kissed him. I averted my eyes, not wanting a front-row seat to their public display of affection.

"I'll see you up in our room." She trailed her fingers across his back and then walked away.

"I should go too," I said, thinking Malachi might be ready to call it a night since he probably needed his rest before tomorrow.

"Jasper, wait." He touched my arm and then pulled his hand away quickly. "We should talk."

I looked around the bar, which was far busier now than when I'd arrived. "This probably isn't the best place to chat."

"Come to my room, then."

"The one you're sharing with Savannah?"

He shook his head. "Just keeping up appearances. Her room is connected to mine, but we have our own space."

"Still, probably not the best idea." I didn't know why I was fighting it when I really did want to go with him.

"Maybe not, but I still want you to."

Unable to say no, I stood and said, "All right."

His lips curved into a small smile, and he quickly led me to his room. My body was buzzing with anticipation, wondering what might happen when we were finally alone.

Once inside, he pushed the door shut behind us and turned to face me. Suddenly, it was like no time had passed, and the desire that was always present when I was near him intensified.

Malachi closed the distance between us and wrapped his hand around the back of my neck. "I've missed you."

"I missed you too."

The second I said the words, his lips were on mine. Our tongues tangled together, and I was immediately transported back in time to when we kissed every chance we got. He guided me toward the bed, but a knock from the connecting room stopped us before we got there.

"Malachi, I heard you come in," Savannah said. "I've got some news to share."

He let out a sigh. "Can it wait until morning?"

"Trust me. You want to hear about this."

"You should go talk to her," I suggested.

He sighed. "Yeah, but we need to talk later."

"Well, you know where to find me." I smiled and then slipped out of his room while he went to Savannah.

14

MALACHI

Banging on my hotel door woke me from a deep sleep. I rolled over, grabbed my pillow, and covered my head with it. The thumping continued.

"Housekeeping!"

I didn't answer, and there was another knock.

"Housekeeping. You want towels?" a fake female voice called out, and I knew exactly who it was.

Getting out of the king-sized bed, I sauntered to the door. Just as I was about to open it, Jesse said again in a phony voice, "Housekeeping. You—"

I swung the door open quickly. "If you want to jerk me off, no need to pretend to be housekeeping," I teased, referring to the scene in the movie *Tommy Boy* that we used to watch all the time when we were younger. It was my dad's favorite and instantly became one of mine too.

"You'd like that, wouldn't you?" Jesse joked back.

"Hell no." He wasn't the Bennett I wanted to touch my dick, anyway. "But why the fuck are you waking me up this early?"

"It's almost noon." He moved past me and into my room.

"And? We don't have sound check for another couple of hours." I closed the door and followed him.

He turned and grinned. "Yeah, well, I need your help."

"Okay?"

"I'm going to propose to Liv tonight during the show."

My eyes widened, and I sucked in a small breath. "No shit?"

"Been wanting to do it for a while and figured what's better than kicking off our tour with a proposal?"

"And if she says no?" I deadpanned.

"We both know that won't happen."

"So, what do you need me to do?"

"This is what I'm thinking …"

As I left the bus after changing into a black sleeveless shirt and jeans after sound check, I sniffed the air and instantly smelled the mouthwatering aroma of Jasper's cooking. I made my way to where my bandmates and the Midnight Thunder guys were gathered around two long tables set up under a canopy and piling their plates high with everything Jasper and Garrett had made for us.

Elliott was the first to dig in as we sat at the table, his face lighting up as he took a bite of the grilled chicken. "Jasper, you've outdone yourself, man. This is incredible."

Jasper grinned, putting a basket of rolls on the table. "Glad you like it. Figured you'd need a good meal before the show."

I took a bite of the chicken and held back a moan. It was fucking grilled perfectly and almost melted in my mouth.

Silas took a bite of his roasted vegetables. "Good? This is the best meal I've had in weeks!"

Jesse clapped Jasper on the shoulder before taking a seat next to me. "Seriously, Jasper. I'm so glad you became a chef."

As the guys continued to praise Jasper and devour his food, I saw an opportunity as he walked away and went to the barbecue where more chicken was grilling. I quickly finished my food and hurried over to him, but as I neared, I saw he was almost frozen in place and I was instantly on high alert.

"What's wrong?" I asked.

"A bee," he breathed.

I scanned the air and spotted the bee as it buzzed near the tray of grilled chicken beside the barbecue.

"Don't move and it will fly away."

"What if I get stung?"

"You won't." I picked up the tray of chicken and moved it to the other side of the plastic table. I grabbed aluminum foil and covered it. The bee flew off. "See?"

Jasper blew out a breath. "Thank you."

"Always." He flipped a few pieces of chicken and then I asked playfully, "So, do you have any more secret recipes you're hiding from us because that chicken is bomb?"

He looked up, a smile tugging at the corner of his mouth. "Maybe a few. Why? You looking for some cooking lessons?"

"Depends," I said, lowering my voice. "Do those lessons come with a naked chef?"

He chuckled, shaking his head. "Maybe."

"Then I want all the private lessons."

Just as Jasper was about to respond, the sound of heels clicking against the pavement drew our attention. Savannah walked over, her eyes flicking between Jasper and me.

"Hey, Malachi," she greeted. "The fans are getting antsy, and we need to give them a little show, remember?"

The night before, her agent had called and told her the game plan for before the concert. She was supposed to go out and do autographs and asked me to go too to play up the boyfriend act for pictures.

I sighed, the moment with Jasper slipping away. "Right. The whole 'happy couple' act."

Savannah looped her arm through mine, something I was quickly learning she did a lot of. "We've got to give the people what they want."

What about what I wanted?

I glanced back at Jasper, who was now focusing intently on the grill. The playful spark in his eyes had dimmed, replaced by a shadow of disappointment. It felt as though a knife had pierced my heart because *he* was who I wanted and it felt as though no matter what, that would never happen. Not only because of Savannah, but also Jesse. While we'd once had a secret relationship, I wasn't sure I wanted that again.

But I wanted him.

"Let's get this over with," I muttered, letting Savannah lead me to where fans had gathered.

We stepped into view of the crowd, the noise level rising as they spotted us. Savannah turned to me, a smile plastered on her face. She wrapped her arms around my neck, pulling me down for a kiss. It was rehearsed and familiar, but it lacked any genuine emotion.

Savannah and I pulled apart, and she kept her smile in place as she whispered, "Thanks for playing along."

"Yeah," I replied, my voice flat. "Anything for the fans."

We signed a few autographs and then walked back to where the rest of the band was waiting. Savannah's hand was still resting on my arm, which was unnecessary since we were now out of public view. The first thing I noticed was that Jasper was gone. I wanted to ask, but couldn't. Instead, I forced a smile and rejoined the group.

"Let's make this a night to remember," Jesse said, raising his energy drink in a toast.

We all cheered and clinked our cans together, but as I raised mine, I couldn't help but glance toward the buses, wondering where Jasper had gone and if I'd get another chance to see him before or after the show.

The roar of the crowd echoed through the theater; the fans were going nuts. We had just finished "Silver Lining," and while our setlist stated it was time for the duet with Savannah, we had a different plan for our first show.

Sweat dripped from every part of my body as I glanced over at Jesse. He gave me a subtle nod. "All right, everyone," I said into my mic. The crowd quieted down slightly. "We've got something special for you tonight."

The audience went wild, probably assuming this was the moment Savannah was going to come out, but of course, it wasn't.

Taking a deep breath, Jesse removed his guitar from his shoulder and handed the instrument to me. His eyes darted briefly to the front row, where Liv stood watching with a bright smile, completely unaware of what was coming next.

Nodding to the guys, I started to strum the chords of the song we'd written together a few years back, a song that had never made it to an album but was perfect for the moment. The lights dimmed, and a single spotlight focused on Jesse as he pulled his mic off the stand and sang, each word full of the love he felt for Olivia.

When he reached the chorus, the music swelled, and I could see Liv's eyes widen in realization. Jesse walked to the edge of the stage with his gaze locked on her. She covered her mouth with her hands.

The crowd, sensing something monumental was about to happen, hushed almost entirely. He stopped singing, and the music faded out. The theater was silent. Jesse knelt at the edge of the stage and pulled out a small black box from his pocket. He opened it, revealing a stunning diamond ring that sparkled under the stage lights.

"Liv," he started. "You are my rock, my best friend, and the love of my life. I can't imagine spending another day without you as my wife. Will you marry me?"

For a split second, everything was still, and then she nodded vigorously, her words lost in the cheers that erupted from the crowd, but I knew she'd said yes.

With a little help from security, she was lifted onto the stage. Jesse stood, slipped the ring onto her finger, then enveloped her in his arms for a deep, passionate kiss. The fans' roar grew louder, and I couldn't help but grin. It was about damn time.

Jesse and Liv pulled apart, both of them beaming. He took her hand and turned back to the audience. "Toronto, she said yes!"

The crowd went wild, and we launched into the next song with Savannah coming out to join me so we could give the fans another love show.

Except ours wasn't real.

IT WAS LATE BY THE TIME WE GOT BACK TO THE HOTEL. NORMALLY WE would be on the buses, heading to the next city, but our next show was less than six hours away, so we chose to spend another night in a bed bigger than the twin we had to endure on the bus.

Everyone went their separate ways, but instead of going to my room, I headed for Jasper's. More than anything, I wanted to know why he missed the concert. I'd expected him to be in the front row next to Olivia, but he wasn't there.

I knocked on the door, and it swung open a few seconds later. I was greeted by a bare-chested Jasper Bennett. My mouth watered as I zeroed in on his six-pack and light dusting of chest hair he didn't have when we were younger.

He looked over his shoulder and then back at me, lowering his voice, "What are you doing here?"

"I wanted to see you."

"Garrett is sleeping."

"Then let's go to my room."

"What if someone sees?"

"They're all crashing. Well, not your brother and Olivia, I bet." I snorted a little laugh. They were definitely fucking, and I wanted to be too.

"Yeah, I bet." He chuckled. "But I don't know. It's risky."

I dug into my pocket and handed him my key, knowing I could use the app on my phone to unlock the door. "Then wait five minutes and come."

He closed his eyes briefly and smiled, probably thinking what I was thinking: if he joined me in my room, we were both going to *come* very soon.

"All right. I'll be there in five."

"Good." I started to walk away but turned back. "Why didn't you stay for the show?"

He furrowed his brow. "I did."

"You weren't with Olivia in the front row," I argued.

"I was backstage with the crew."

I nodded; that made sense. "Okay, but next show, I want you in the front row."

"We'll see." He winked and shut the door.

I smirked as I walked to the elevator and hit the UP button. I was still smiling as I reached my room and went inside. Hell, I was still grinning when, not even five minutes later, my hotel door started to open.

Pulling it, I reached out and grabbed Jasper's hand. As soon as the lock clicked behind him, we went at it like we were starved for each other. Before long, we were both naked, all our clothes scattered on the floor.

"I've been thinking about this for weeks," I admitted.

"Me too," he panted.

We fell onto the bed, kissing and caressing, both of our dicks hard as stone. I moved to straddle his leg and took one of his nipples into my mouth. His back arched as he hissed out a moan. Twirling my tongue around the peak, I looked up at him with hooded eyes. Just the sight of how much he was enjoying what I was doing to him, hit me straight in the feels. I had missed him so much and now I was going to do everything to him I had fantasized about over the years.

I kissed him once again and then trailed my lips down his hard chest, kissing a path toward his dick. At the same time, I fisted his cock, giving it a few pumps and rolling his balls in my hand.

"Fuck," Jasper groaned.

I lifted my head and asked, "You want me to suck your big dick?"

"God, yes," he breathed.

Without any hesitation, I engulfed his length, sucking and twirling until the tip of him hit the back of my throat. His moans spurred me on as I devoured him, tasting the first few drops of pre-cum as my tongue slid across his crown while I bobbed.

He grabbed my hand that wasn't wrapped around his base and pulled it until my fingers grazed his lips. His mouth opened, and he sucked on my digits, matching what I was doing to his cock. My dick throbbed as I moved my hips against his leg and the tip leaked drops of my own arousal.

"You suck me better than I remember," Jasper gasped.

I popped off his length and pumped him with my hand. "Yeah? You like this?"

"Fuck, yeah, but I want you inside of me."

"You gonna let me fuck you bareback so I can feel all of you?"

"Yeah, I'm on PrEP. Fuck me all you want."

I grinned, liking that idea. "I'm on it too."

Our mouths were like magnets as we kissed again and if I wasn't inside him soon, the hotel bed was going to be covered with my cum and not dripping from his hole like I wanted it to be.

"Roll over," I said against his lips.

He turned, getting onto his stomach.

"You know what I've wanted to do but never got the chance?" I asked as I kissed down his back.

"What's that?" He looked over his shoulder at me.

I grabbed his ass, spreading his cheeks and diving in with my tongue.

"Oh god," he growled and planted his face into the comforter.

I hummed a response as I swirled his puckered rim, eating him like he was my last meal.

Jasper's hips rocked against the mattress, his pants and groans making me not want to wait any longer.

I hurried off the bed, got the lube, and popped the cap in a flash. Squirting it onto my palm, I coated my dick with the thick liquid and then returned to my place between his legs. Taking the bottle, I held it above his perfect ass and poured it into his crack, watching it run down and over the rosebud that was waiting to be filled.

"I can't wait to see my cum leaking out of you."

"Then fuck me already, Malachi."

"Fuck, I love it when you're demanding."

I lined up behind him as he lifted his ass into the air and then spread the lube around his hole and slipped a finger inside. Jasper moaned, his hips jerking forward, and he was tighter than I thought he'd be. He was going to feel so fucking good.

Adding another finger, I stretched him some more before I nudged my tip against his opening.

"I've never fucked anyone bare before," I admitted, feeling him squeeze the head of my cock. It was the truth. While I was on the medication to keep me healthy since I had been known to fuck a lot, I never went without a condom. Not until now. Not until *him*.

"I never have either," he responded.

I leaned forward and took his lips again, my dick sliding in a little further. "I love having firsts with you."

"Me too," he moaned against my lips and then gasped as I filled him completely.

"Jesus Christ, Jasper. I missed watching my dick slide into you."

I tried to go slow, rocking a little as I made sure to hit the spot that felt so good. But with each drive, my body screamed at me to go harder. To pound into him while he held on for dear life. And that was what I did.

I grabbed his hips and drove into him, making the bed squeak and hit the wall with each thrust. We were both moaning and groaning, and I didn't care if Savannah—whose room was on the other side of the wall—could hear us. All I cared about was finally being with Jasper Bennett again. If I had my way, it wasn't going to be the only time.

As we got closer to coming, I wanted to watch his face as he exploded with me inside of him.

As if he was thinking the same thing, he turned onto his back when I slid out of him. We stared at each other as he widened his legs and I sank into him.

I tried to fuck him slowly again, taking his mouth with mine, but instead, he grabbed my ass and urged me to go faster. I did, rocking into him over and over. I saw his hand wrap around his dick and start to pump himself.

Grabbing his leg, I draped it over my shoulder so I could go deeper. His head tilted back on a moan as he continued to fuck his fist.

"I'm close," I said.

"I'm almost there too."

He was closer than I thought because not even a minute later, ropes of cum squirted from his cock and onto his stomach.

"Fuck," I groaned, moving faster and chasing him. With only a few more thrusts, my balls drew up, and I unloaded into him.

Once I was spent, I slid out of him, watching my cum run down between his cheeks like I wanted. It was a sight I was going to remember while in my bunk on the tour bus when everyone else was sleeping and all I could do was think about my best friend's brother on the bus behind ours.

Since I hadn't gotten to taste all of him, I licked his jizz off his abs as I kissed my way up to his mouth. He didn't hesitate to open for me. After a few moments, I got up and grabbed a few tissues for him to clean up with. I was worried that if he got out of the bed, he would leave and I wasn't ready for him to go back to his room.

"Remember the first time we were in a hotel together?" I asked as I slid next to him on my side facing him.

"How could I forget? It was my first time having sex."

"Mine too, with a guy."

"I remember."

I lightly grazed the crescent tattoo on his wrist with my finger. "How are you liking life on the road so far?"

"A lot better than I expected."

"What do you mean?" My brow furrowed.

"Nothing." He turned his head to look at the wall next to us.

"Did you think you weren't going to like the job?" I wondered.

"No, I knew I'd like that part."

"Then what was it?"

Letting out a deep sigh, he looked back at me. "I was afraid of seeing you again."

I balked slightly. "You were? Why?"

He shrugged but didn't answer.

"C'mon, you can't say that and then not explain."

"You really want to know?"

"Of course."

"Because seeing you had the potential to make me fall in love with you again."

"Again?"

He nodded, and my breath caught. He had been in love with me? Back then, I thought I only had love *for* him, but after winning *The Band Showdown* and knowing he was going to Paris, I had realized I was missing him because I was *in* love with him. I'd tried to fight my feelings and tell myself it wasn't true, but I found over the years that when I wrote songs, most of the lyrics were about him.

He continued. "I knew back then what we had could never be more than a secret relationship, but that didn't stop me from falling in love with you."

It was on the tip of my tongue to tell him I was in love with him too, but instead, I sealed my lips against his and got in another round before he had to go back to his room so no one caught him sneaking out of mine.

15

JASPER

WE WERE ON OUR WAY TO MONTREAL AND MY MIND WAS A JUMBLED mess from the night before. While the night before had been amazing, it had also left me with a lot of questions. Were we rekindling something and going to be together again? Had it been a one-time thing? Were we going back to sneaking around like we had when we were younger?

I also couldn't forget how I admitted I had been in love with him years ago. It wasn't as though I had planned to tell him, but when he'd asked me what I had been worried about, I'd felt as though I owed him the truth. What I didn't say though was those feelings were rushing back much faster than I expected.

"So, what's the plan today?" Garrett asked as he sat across from me while we rolled down the highway.

Besides Garrett and me, eight other people traveled with us. Our bus had a kitchen, a small dining table where we were currently sitting, and a couple of couches at the front. In the middle were twelve twin-sized bunk beds, and just past that, there was another entertaining area with a wraparound couch. It was a tight fit, but getting to travel and see new places made it all worth it.

"After lunch, we need to make another grocery run. I've got a list of all the snacks everyone likes, and we'll buy everything for tonight and tomorrow and start working on the large crew dinner when we get back."

Since it was a show night, we would be cooking for a crowd. Preparing food on the road was a lot different from doing it in a home or restaurant. One of the vans traveling with us, towed a mobile kitchen we would use to make most of our meals. One of the biggest challenges was storing the cold items we purchased. Even though the trailer had a large refrigerator inside, I didn't want to risk the generator not working properly while traveling and losing a bunch of food in the process. Instead, I decided we would make frequent trips to the store to buy what we needed and keep it all in the fridge on the bus.

As soon as we pulled into the theater parking lot, I started grabbing the sandwich fixings I'd bought before we'd left Toronto. Rina told us to expect things to move quickly when we got to our location, so an easy lunch seemed like a good idea.

Once the driver parked, Garrett and I followed everyone off of the bus. Rina headed over to the one the band was on and climbed aboard while we helped the local theater crew, who were waiting to help us set up the canopy and tables.

While we scrambled around to get everything ready, the door to Surrender's bus opened, and the guys spilled out. Olivia was the last off as Jesse offered his hand to help her down the steps. Watching them, I couldn't help the small amount of jealousy that rose up inside me because they didn't have to worry about what others thought about their relationship and were free to show their love for each other openly. Something I might never be able to do with Malachi even if we started things up again.

I glanced over at him and he winked. Were we starting things up again?

After lunch, there was a flurry of activity as the crew got to work. The guys were still sitting around the table when Jesse waved me over. I took the open spot next to Elliott, which put me directly across from Malachi.

"We're gonna go check out the city a bit before we have to get ready for tonight. You want to join us?" my brother asked.

It would be nice to hang out with them, but I had a full afternoon ahead of me. "Sounds like fun, but Garrett and I have a bunch of stuff to take care of."

"I know you've got a job to do, but we want you to have a good time as well," Elliott said.

Jesse nodded. "All work and no play isn't good for anybody."

I glanced at Malachi, who was trying to hide a smirk, and I wondered if he was thinking about how much we had played the night before. I was pretty sure I got my answer when he brushed his foot against mine.

Averting my gaze because I worried the smile I felt creep across my face might give me away, I turned to the rest of the group and said, "Once I get my bearings, I promise I'll get out a bit and explore."

"Good." Jesse stood and held out a hand to Olivia. "We should get going so we make it back in time for sound check. Don't need Rina busting our balls this early on the tour."

The guys laughed and got up to head to the bus.

"See you later, Jasper." Malachi winked and then followed the others.

After the guys headed out, Garrett and I left to go shopping, where the small amount of French I had retained from my time in Paris came in handy, seeing as it was the primary language spoken in the city.

When we returned, only a handful of security guards were around. We flashed them our credentials and then started unloading the vehicle we had borrowed for our errands.

Once everything was organized, I grabbed the bags of snacks. "I'm going to put these on the other bus. Can you get started on dinner prep?"

Garrett nodded. "No problem."

It took a moment for my eyes to adjust to the darkened interior of the guys' bus. It looked similar to ours but, from what I could tell, had only six bunk beds, giving them each a little more space than what we had.

I began separating the snacks into the baskets I'd purchased. They each got their own, including Olivia, and I filled them with the items they had told me they liked. Most of it was sugar-filled crap. It was a good thing they had me around to make them some nutritious meals since they clearly still ate like teenagers.

While looking for space in the cabinets to store everything, I felt someone grab my ass, causing me to jump and spin around to see that it was Malachi. "What are you doing here? I thought you were going out."

He pressed a light kiss to my lips and then said, "I wanted to see you, so I left early and told the guys I was going to grab a nap before sound check."

"When will they be back?" I asked breathily as he trailed kisses down my neck.

He reached for the button on my jeans. "Soon, I would guess."

"Maybe you shouldn't be trying to get to my dick if you don't want us to get caught." I chuckled but made no attempt to stop him.

"Or you could stop asking questions and just let me blow you."

I was never one to resist Malachi Danvers. Every time we were together, it carried a risk someone might find out about us, but when his hands moved down to my zipper, I threw all caution to the wind.

"You better be quick then."

He dropped to his knees. In a flash, he undid my fly and pushed my jeans down to my thighs. He fisted my hardening dick and flicked his tongue against the sensitive area on the underside of my cock. The feeling of his wet tongue on me caused me to lean against the refrigerator behind me, my head thudding against the door.

He licked up and down my length while gently tugging on my balls with his free hand. With each pass of his mouth, I expected him to start sucking me off, but he continued taking his time torturing me.

I looked down at him. "You're such a tease."

"You love it." His gaze met mine and he smiled before he returned his focus to my throbbing erection. He may have been the one on his knees, but he had full control of the moment.

"Please," I rasped.

"Please, what?" He slid his hand from my balls and up my crack, lightly tapping my hole. "Tell me what you want."

"Wrap your lips around me and swallow my cock until I come."

"Well, since you asked so nicely..." A devilish glint shined in his eyes as he opened his mouth and engulfed my shaft. My fingers twisted in his hair, and I couldn't stop my hips from thrusting forward. "That's it. Fuck my mouth," he groaned as I pulled back, then drove back in, feeling my dick hit the back of his throat.

My heart raced as he worked me over. "Yes, just like that," I gasped. "Don't stop."

He hummed, the only sign he heard me.

Smoothing his hand up my stomach and chest, he pressed his fingertips against my lips, urging me to open. I did and started to mimic what he was doing to my cock, coating his digits with my saliva.

Just when I thought it couldn't get any better, he pulled his fingers free and slipped a spit-covered digit deep inside me, rubbing against the spot that had me seeing stars.

"Oh god," I gasped.

He fingered my ass faster while he sucked and bobbed his head. My legs felt as though they were going to give out as I was on the brink. Tightening my grip in his hair, I rocked my hips against his face. "I'm gonna come."

He sucked me harder, and within seconds my dick was jerking as I shot streams of hot cum down his throat. I fell back against the fridge again, trying to catch my breath as he milked me dry.

Malachi pulled off me and stood. "You good?"

"Yeah, that was ... Wow," I stammered.

He chuckled. "Glad you enjoyed it because I plan on doing that every chance I get." His mouth descended on mine.

Lost in his kiss that tasted like my cum, it took a second for the sound of the door opening to register in my brain. Luckily, Malachi must have heard it, because he tore his mouth away from mine and plopped down on the couch. I had just enough time to turn away from the front of the bus and tuck my dick back inside my jeans before the rest of the band came on board.

"Hey, bro. Whatcha doing?" Jesse asked when he noticed me standing in the small kitchen area.

"I bought some stuff for you guys to have in here," I explained, hoping he didn't pick up on how breathless I sounded. "You each have your own basket."

"Awesome." Silas reached for his bag of Jolly Ranchers.

"Thanks, man." Elliott clapped my shoulder as he passed by on his way to the bunk beds.

"No problem. I'm going to finish making dinner. It'll be ready when you guys finish your sound check."

"Great. See you in a bit." Jesse led Olivia toward the back.

"Later," Malachi called out as I climbed down the steps.

"Later." I echoed back and then shut the door behind me.

Leaning against the side of the bus, I closed my eyes and let out a deep breath. That had been close. Too close, really. After taking a moment to collect myself, I opened my eyes again, only to find Savannah staring directly at me.

16

MALACHI

I wasn't really one to date. Sex? Yes. But to take someone to dinner, a movie, whatever, hadn't been my speed for a long time. However, I had to pretend to be dating Savannah because everyone had been on my ass the last two weeks to play up the boyfriend thing.

So, when we had a free day in Winnipeg, she and I headed to a restaurant for a *date*. Everyone else had a day to do whatever the fuck they wanted—and the guys were doing just that—but I wasn't so lucky. If I could have, I would've taken someone else out to dinner.

Okay, maybe I wasn't against dating, but rather the person I wanted to date wasn't Savannah Sky. Except being seen out with Jasper wouldn't be good with Jesse, Stellar Records, or the fans. The internet was buzzing about me and Savannah, speculating if I was going to be the next one to propose during a concert.

As Savannah and I stepped out of the car, the flash of cameras nearly blinded me. Paparazzi had been following us since we'd left the hotel, and I could feel their eyes boring into my back as we made our way into the Italian restaurant. True to her style, Savannah looped her arm through mine, and waved to the cameras, clearly putting on a show.

We were seated at a table by the window, a prime spot for photographers to get their shots. If we were on an actual date, I would have made sure we sat in the back and out of sight of anyone, but since it was all for publicity, everything had to be on display. Same with the smile on my face, though it wasn't genuine.

A waitress came over and we ordered a bottle of shiraz. It wasn't my go-to but nothing was lately. I felt as though none of my actions were truly me. Except, of course, when I had seen Jasper get on our bus alone and I'd followed him inside and blew him. That was fun.

"I can't wait to get back in the studio and record my next album," Savannah said, but instead of replying, my gaze wandered out the window, imagining what it would be like to be here with Jasper instead.

We could have been laughing over some inside joke, his hand brushing against mine as we reached for the same piece of bread. But instead, I was here, playing the perfect boyfriend for someone I didn't love.

Love?

Was I in love with Jasper?

As I sat there, sipping the red wine, I couldn't deny that a part of me had always loved him. And I wished I could wrap my arms around him and kiss him without having to hide how I felt about him. I wanted everyone to know I was with a guy and not have to fake a relationship with a chick I had sung a duet with—a song I'd written about Jasper, the man I loved. Yeah, I was totally still fucking in love with him.

"Malachi?" Savannah's voice pulled me out of my thoughts. "Are you even listening?"

"Yeah, sorry," I mumbled, taking another sip of my wine. "Just tired."

"I know you don't date, but I feel like I'm the one making this sham of a relationship work." She gave me a sympathetic look, but I could see the frustration behind her eyes. She knew this was a charade just as well as I did; we both had our roles to play. The fans wanted a romance, so we had to give them one, even if it was a lie.

I lifted a shoulder. "What do you want from me?"

"You're amazing on stage, playing up the rock star persona. I know you can fake it."

"I don't play up the rock star persona, Savvy. Music is in my blood."

"I get it, but you need to give me something to work with here."

I took a deep breath and then reached for her hand, playing with her fingers as the cameras outside continued to fire. Doing what needed to be done, we talked and laughed, and I suppose from the outside, it looked as though we were on a date. The paparazzi never let up, capturing every bogus moment of affection.

Once dinner was done, we headed back to the hotel we were staying in. As we entered the lobby, I spotted Jasper near the elevators talking with one of the crew. Our eyes met briefly, and he gave me a tight smile. Was this killing him as much as it was me?

Taking my phone out of my pocket, I sent him a text as the elevator ascended to my floor.

> Come to my room

THE NEXT DAY AFTER SOUND CHECK, I WAS THE LAST TO HEAD TOWARD the buses. We were going to catch some sleep before the show, and since I had been up late the night before, I was looking forward to a little nap. Except as I made my way across the lot, I spotted Jasper leaning against the side of one of the tour buses, engrossed in his phone.

"Hey," I greeted him, glancing around to make sure we were alone. "You good?"

"Yep—"

I pulled him to the back of the bus and closed the distance between us, his hands immediately going to my waist and bringing me against his body as I pinned him against the metal.

"I hate waking up and you're gone," I admitted against his lips.

"I know," he replied. "But I have to slip out when no one will catch me."

Just as our lips met again, I heard a sharp intake of breath. We sprang apart, and I turned to see Savannah standing a few feet away, her eyes wide with shock.

"Savannah ..." I began.

She crossed her arms, looking between Jasper and me. "Wow. I'm shocked."

"You can't tell anyone," I pleaded.

"Why would I? That would mess up our phony relationship."

"Yeah," I agreed and glanced at Jasper. He looked as though he was ready to bolt at any second. I didn't blame him.

"Does Jesse know?" she asked.

I shook my head. "No. He would flip."

"How long has this been going on?" she inquired.

"Since ..." I hesitated and looked at Jasper again. "Since forever."

"Forever?"

I grabbed Jasper's hand and squeezed it before letting it go. "We had a thing back when I lived in Boston."

To my surprise, Savannah's expression softened. "Wow. I mean, I knew something was off, but ... wow. You really had me fooled."

Jasper stepped forward. "Savannah, please don't tell anyone, especially my brother."

"Also no one knows I'm bi, and I'm not ready to deal with the fallout from that announcement," I added.

She let out a breath. "I get it now. It all makes sense. You have matching tattoos and all." She paused, then looked at Jasper with a hint of a smile. "Holy shit. 'Whispers in the Night' is about you, huh?"

I nodded to her, then grinned at him. "Yeah, it is."

"Really?" he asked, looking back at me.

"Of course, it is." I winked.

"Aw, that's so cute, and honestly, I thought maybe you just hated being around me."

"Savvy, no," I breathed. "It's not you at all."

She sighed, a small laugh escaping her lips. "Well, at least I don't have to worry about you getting mad that I have feelings for Elliott."

"Wait. What?" I balked.

"We've been secretly ... Well, probably doing the same as you two."

"Really?" I had no idea. I knew he'd taken her home the night I turned her down after Jasper arrived in LA, but I had no clue they meant anything to each other.

Jasper chuckled and asked, "So, you're okay with this?"

Savannah nodded slowly. "I am and maybe we can come up with a plan together to make all our relationships work."

Except that meant telling Elliott I was bi and with Jasper. "We can't tell Elliott."

"Oh." Savannah's shoulders sagged. "Right."

"But I'm cool with keeping up the ruse for as long as we need to. Maybe after the tour, we can have our fake breakup and then you and Elliott can be together in public," I suggested.

"Or we can create some sort of cheating scandal. Everyone loves a scandal," she countered.

"If you and Elliott want to do that, then we can discuss it," I said. "But I'm not ready for him or the other guys to find out about me and Jasper. Especially Jesse. He will flip."

"Why?" Savannah questioned. "If you two are happy, then shouldn't he be happy for you?"

"In theory." I lifted a shoulder. "But I don't think telling him while we're mid-tour is the best plan, just in case."

"All right." She nodded. "I need to go get a little beauty sleep and I suggest you two stop making out behind the buses where everyone can see."

"Thanks." As Savannah walked away, I said to Jasper, "That went better than I expected."

He nodded. "It did."

He started to walk away, but I grabbed his wrist. "What's wrong?"

"Just thinking."

"About?"

"Jesse," Jasper replied.

"About telling him?" I dropped his wrist.

He nodded. "Yeah. I don't know. I feel like we're back when I was in high school. Jesse shouldn't care who I date."

"I agree, but it's not just that. No one knows I'm bi."

"I know." He looked down at the asphalt.

"But I think Savannah's right," I continued. "We can't keep sneaking around forever. We just have to figure out the right time and way to tell them."

"You want to come out?"

"If it means we can be together, then yeah."

A smile tugged at his lips. "You want to be together?"

"Isn't it obvious?"

"Now it is."

I pulled him closer and brushed my lips against his ear as I whispered, "Good, because I want everyone to know you're mine."

Just then, Savannah reappeared, a playful smirk on her face. She didn't say anything, and Jasper and I pulled apart. The weight of our secret felt a little lighter, knowing we had an ally in her.

Before we parted ways, I tugged Jasper in for one last quick kiss. "I want you in my bed again tonight," I whispered.

"I'll be there," he replied, and we walked to our respective buses.

As I climbed into my bunk, I imagined a future with Jasper, one where we didn't have to hide. But could that ever be? Just because Savannah was cool with it, didn't mean Jesse would be.

17

Jasper

After Winnipeg, the guys played four more shows including ones in Edmonton and Calgary. We were on our way to Vancouver for the last stop on the Canadian leg of the tour.

One of the hard things about living on the road was Malachi and I had trouble finding time to be alone. It seemed as though we were always surrounded by people, so we were limited to me sneaking in and out of his hotel room at all hours of the night or stealing kisses behind the bus.

Just like how it had been when we were younger.

That didn't mean I wasn't having the time of my life. I'd taken Elliott's and my brother's advice and had joined them for some sightseeing whenever my schedule allowed it. It still sucked having to pretend Malachi and I were only friends when we'd go out.

I was sitting at the small dining table with Garrett and Rina, scrolling on my phone while the rest of the crew traveling with us were sprawled across the couches or in their beds. I had just opened one of my social media apps when a text from Malachi popped up on the screen.

> Whatcha doing?

> Just checking out social media. What about you?

> Lying in bed. Thinking about last night

> Any part in particular? 😏

As had become our routine, I'd spent the night in his hotel room after the concert. He'd given me a key earlier in the day, and while the band was busy with their meet and greet, I'd snuck in and waited naked for him when he came back.

> Just how much I enjoyed being buried balls deep in your ass

My dick stiffened and pressed painfully against my zipper. "I'm going to grab a nap before we roll up to the theater," I said to Garrett and Rina, who were both focused on their phones and completely oblivious to the dirty messages I was receiving.

Garrett nodded. "Cool. I think I'll do the same."

"I'll wake you guys up when we get there," Rina replied.

I made my way to my bunk and climbed inside, pulling the curtain closed to give myself a little privacy.

> You can't text me things like that when I'm around other people. LOL I have a massive hard-on now

> Go to your bunk, and I'll show you what thinking about being deep inside of you does to me

I swallowed and typed back:

> Already there

A second later, I was staring at a photo of Malachi's huge erection. I adjusted myself, giving my dick a little squeeze.

> Fuck ... I hate that I have to wait until I get you alone again

> Oh yeah? And what do you plan to do with me?

I groaned, and Garrett called out from the bed beneath mine. "You okay up there?"

"Yep. Just bumped my head," I lied.

> I'm waiting ...

> Keep your pants on

> I think the pic I sent shows it's too late for that. So going back to my question. What would you do if we were alone?

I'd never sexted before, and a thrill shot through me as I imagined making Malachi come with only my words.

> I would take my time peeling off every piece of clothing from your gorgeous body. Then I'd trail my tongue over every inch of you, teasing you until you begged me to suck your dick

> Your mouth IS incredible

I could practically taste his pre-cum on my taste buds as I pictured myself going down on him.

> Eventually, I'd give in to your demand and sink to my knees, deep throating you until I couldn't breathe

> I love it when you choke on my cock. Watching your eyes water as you choose my dick over oxygen has me ready to explode every time

I shoved my pants down my thighs, licked my palm, and fisted my shaft, giving it a hard tug.

> Yeah, but I wouldn't let you come

> You wouldn't?

I slid my hand up and down myself as I texted with one hand:

> At least not in my mouth

> Where would you want it then?

> In my ass. I'd climb up on the bed, and you'd fuck me from behind

> I'd pound you so hard everyone on our floor would hear you scream my name

Holy shit. I stroked myself faster, spreading my pre-cum all over my shaft.

> I can feel your tight ass clenching around me as I fill your hole with my cum

> I'm going to come

I lifted my shirt and threw my pillow over my face to muffle my moans as I sprayed my load all over my stomach.

> Me too

> I want to see

A moment later, he sent a photo of his cock with cum dripping down his length. I desperately wanted to lick it off of him.

> Your turn

I held up my phone and snapped a pic of me covered in my release and sent it.

> Damn that's sexy. I want to lick it off of you
>
> I wish we could help clean each other up
>
> You'll get your chance tonight

AFTER WE ARRIVED AT THE THEATER IN VANCOUVER, GARRETT started lunch. Once he confirmed he had everything under control, I got ready to go to the store. Since it was a show night, we needed to get the groceries early so we had enough time to cook before a couple dozen band and crew members got hangry.

Keys in hand, I hit the unlock button on the remote as I headed over to the SUV. I was about to climb in when someone stopped me with a hand on my arm.

"Where are you off to?" Malachi asked.

"I need to pick up some groceries. Do you want to come with me?" It's not like we could go on a date, but I would take whatever time I could with him.

He grinned. "Yeah, just give me a minute."

I didn't stop myself from checking out his ass as he jogged toward his bus.

"You got it bad," Savannah giggled, appearing out of nowhere.

"Do you have some sort of superpower that helps you sneak up on people?" I teased.

"No. You were just so focused on his ass, you didn't hear me approach."

Over the past couple of weeks, she had kept her promise not to tell anyone since she caught us kissing and had become someone I considered a friend. Even though she'd had a piece of my man at one point.

My man.

I smiled at the thought.

"See." She pointed at me, a gleam in her eye. "I'd bet good money you're thinking about him right now."

I shrugged and laughed. "You'd be right."

A few seconds later, Malachi headed back our way with a hat pulled down over his head.

"Where are you going?" Jesse called out from the table he was sitting at with Olivia.

"I need to pick up a few things at the store, so I'm hitching a ride with Jasper," Malachi shouted back.

"Have fun." Savannah winked and walked away.

"Do you want to drive?" I asked, holding up the keys.

Since I preferred using public transportation over driving, I would always pick being a passenger instead of driving.

"Sure." He took the keys from my hand.

We got into the SUV, and I typed the address into the GPS. As soon as we were on the road, he laced his fingers with mine and rested our joined hands on my thigh.

"Did you really need to get something at the store, or was that an excuse to come with me?"

He glanced my way and arched a brow. "What do you think?"

"Too bad we can't go shopping every day."

He squeezed my hand. "Yeah, but I was thinking, when we're in LA, maybe we can come up with a plan for you to spend the night at my place."

We would be back in LA in a little more than a week, and I could feel myself getting hard just thinking about all the trouble we could get up to for an entire night without worrying about getting caught.

"I'd like that."

"Good." He rubbed the backside of my thumb with his.

When we got to the store, we made sure to keep our distance. Even though Malachi was wearing a hat, he wasn't invisible. It was likely some of the customers were aware Surrender was in town and might easily recognize him.

Once I had a cart full of groceries, I headed to the checkout. "You should probably grab a few things while we're here, so Jesse doesn't realize you were full of shit," I teased.

"You're right. I'll meet you out at the car in a few minutes." He handed me the keys.

I had loaded the last bag into the trunk when he came out. He tossed his stuff inside and we climbed in to take off. Just as he had before, he reached over and grabbed my hand.

"It sucks not being able to touch you when we're in public," he grumbled.

"Don't worry, you'll be able to touch me all you want in your hotel room after the show." I waggled my eyebrows.

"I don't think I can wait that long."

"It's not like we have any other choice—"

"Yeah, but I'm still worked up from our sexting earlier." Before I knew what was happening, he pulled into the parking lot for a park that overlooked the bay and found a secluded corner. "Let's go."

"Go? Where?"

He opened the door and moved to the back of the SUV. When I joined him, he was pushing the groceries to one side and folding down the seats. "Get in." I did as he said, and he crawled in behind me. After he closed the liftgate, he rummaged through one of the bags and pulled out a bottle of lube. "Now take off your pants."

18

MALACHI

One thing I loved about California was the weather; most of the time, it was perfect. Rina knew what she was doing when she scheduled us to have our shows in LA in mid-May.

Los Angeles was also the first place on the tour where we would play back-to-back shows, and then we'd get a little bit of a break before we headed down to San Diego to continue our tour. The only thing better would have been to wake up with Jasper in my bed, but that would have to wait until tomorrow because we'd planned for him to come over after tonight's show.

The sun hung high over Jesse's backyard where we were going to have a quick meal before heading to our sound check. The smell of grilled meat mingled with the sweet scent of blooming jasmine as I stepped through the side gate. Jasper stood by the grill, and my heart skipped a beat the moment I saw him. His dark purple T-shirt clung to his back, damp with sweat, and I had to force myself to look away before anyone noticed me staring at him.

"Malachi, grab a beer and come here for a second," Jesse called from the deck, raising a cold one in my direction. Olivia sat beside him, her face buried in a bridal magazine.

"All right, be right there," I replied, walking over to Jasper, thankful the cooler was next to him. "Smells amazing."

He glanced up, his eyes locking with mine for a fraction of a second longer than necessary. "Thanks. Just trying not to overcook it. It's my first time grilling tri-tip."

"Looks good to me," I said, and it took everything in me not to kiss him. Instead, I reached into the ice chest and grabbed a bottle of Stella.

"Guess we'll find out." He winked.

"Don't flirt with me or everyone will find out our secret because I won't be able to stop myself any longer from kissing you."

"As soon as I pull this meat off, you can meet me in the kitchen. I might need help in the pantry."

"You're alone?" I asked, because I thought maybe his cooking buddy might be helping him.

"Yeah. Told Garrett I could handle a little barbecue for you guys, so he's out sightseeing."

"Ah. Well, I better go see what your brother wants." I hooked my thumb in Jesse's direction. "But I'll meet you in the kitchen."

"Okay. Everything will be ready soon."

I gave Jasper a little smile and then headed over to Jesse and Olivia. Sitting by the pool, Elliott and Savannah caught my eye. Elliott leaned in close to her and whispered something that made Savannah bite her bottom lip. She swatted his arm playfully and laughed. Luckily it was just the immediate band—well, besides Silas—hanging out, so Savannah and I didn't need to pretend to be dating. She and Elliott could do whatever they wanted.

"Where's Silas?" I asked as I took a seat next to Jesse.

He lifted a shoulder. "I don't know. He hasn't arrived yet."

"Maybe stuck in traffic, then." I took a pull of my beer.

"Maybe," Jesse replied. "But enough about him. I want to ask you something."

"All right. Shoot."

A huge smile spread across his face. "Want to be my best man?"

I blinked. "Me? What about your brother?"

"After the tour, he'll be back in Boston. Plus, you're my best friend and you can plan shit I like better."

"Like what?"

"The bachelor party and stuff." Jesse lifted a shoulder.

"No strippers," Olivia chimed in, not looking up from her magazine but clearly listening.

Jesse rolled his eyes. "Right. No strippers."

"All right, I'll be your best man."

"Great. Also, Liv's staying behind when we leave for San Diego. She wants to work on all the wedding stuff."

"Yep," she replied. "Tons of details to iron out. But I'll catch up with you guys in Boston and go to the last few shows."

LA and Boston were the only cities where we had back-to-back shows. After Boston, we would end the tour in New York City. It was still a few months away, and I liked the thought of spending every day with Jasper while *doing* what I loved each night: him and singing.

"All right. Did you set a date?"

"Not yet, but we're thinking next May." Jesse smiled at his fiancée.

"Cool. Gives me time to plan something epic for your last night as a single man."

Jesse grinned, but before he could respond, a sudden yelp pierced the air. I whipped my head around to see Jasper clutching his arm, his eyes wide as he stared at us. Instantly, my heart leaped into my throat.

"Shit!" I shouted, rushing to his side. "What's wrong?"

He doubled over as he clenched his bicep. "A fucking bee stung me."

"Hang on, man. I'll get your EpiPen," Jesse called out, his voice calm but urgent as he bolted into the house.

I knelt beside Jasper as Olivia, Savannah, and Elliott stood back and watched. "Jasper, look at me," I said, my voice soft. I wanted to reach out and lift his chin, but I held back. "You're gonna be okay."

"Yeah, but why is it always me?"

"It's because you're too sweet," I whispered.

He snorted a laugh and sat on the concrete. "Fuckers just want to kill me."

"We won't let that happen."

Jesse returned quickly, and after he stuck Jasper in the leg with the medication, he said, "We need to get him to the ER."

"You guys have your show," Jasper protested. "I'll be fine."

"I'll take you," Olivia stated.

I looked up at her. "Are you sure?"

"Of course. I'll go get my keys."

"Thanks, baby." Jesse kissed the side of her head.

Everyone except me dispersed, and I sat next to Jasper as we waited for the medication to fully get into his system.

"Remember when you got stung when we went camping?" I asked.

"How could I forget?" He chuckled slightly. "We had our first kiss that night."

"Yeah, we did." I smirked, remembering that night.

"I was so scared, though, when you got stung. Still am."

"I'll be fine," Jasper assured me.

"Probably so, but it still doesn't make my heart hurt any less."

"You say that as though you love me."

Out of sight from everyone, I brushed his pinky with mine. "I do."

Jasper's gaze collided with mine. "You do?"

"I should have told you when you admitted to me that you were in love with me back in the day. I don't know why I didn't, but yes, Jasper 'The Best Chef Ever' Bennett, I love you and you really need to stop getting stung because it's killing me."

He smiled softly. "I love you too."

I was seconds away from leaning over and kissing him, but Jesse returned.

"We actually called an ambulance instead, and it's on its way. Figured it's better to be safe," he stated.

Jasper rolled his eyes. "You guys worry too much."

"Can't help it." I nudged him gently with my shoulder. "You're kinda important to us."

"Yeah, well, not sure a ride in an ambulance is necessary."

"The paramedics will check you out, and make sure your medication is working, but you know you need to see a doctor too," Olivia said.

"I know, but an ambulance?" he argued.

"This LA traffic is no joke," I cut in. "It will get you to the hospital faster than Olivia can drive."

"All right, fine, but I need to get the tri-tip and Savannah's black bean burger off the grill before they burn."

"I got it." I stood and grabbed the tongs and the plate Jasper had sitting on the side. After I took the burger and meat off, I said, "There. The tri-tip needs to rest, right?"

"Yeah, thank you." Jasper smiled up at me and I grinned back.

The paramedics arrived a few minutes later and quickly took over. After the EMTs checked him out, Jasper walked to the ambulance, then got on the stretcher inside. I knew he was going to be okay, but seeing him going to the hospital still made me a little stressed.

Olivia stepped forward. "I'll go with him. You guys need to get to sound check soon."

I hesitated, my protective instincts battling with my responsibilities. Jesse clapped a hand on my shoulder. "She's right. We have a show to get ready for."

I nodded, giving Olivia a grateful smile. "Take care of him."

"Of course," she replied, climbing into the ambulance beside Jasper.

Jesse, Elliott, Savannah, and I watched as the ambulance drove away. The moment it turned the corner, Jesse spun to us. "We should get moving if we're going to make it to sound check on time."

I hadn't even realized how much time had passed while the EMTs were here.

"Hold on," Elliott said. "We've got a few minutes, and we need to eat something before we go."

"Yeah, we don't want to perform on an empty stomach," Savannah stated. "Plus, we can't let Jasper's good cooking go to waste."

Jesse nodded. "Good thinking."

In no time, the food was laid out on the kitchen island inside, and we all grabbed plates, loading them up with the tri-tip, pasta salad, and rolls Jasper had made from scratch.

Silas still hadn't arrived, and I briefly wondered if he'd show up at the concert at all. It wasn't like him not to, but then again, on the road, our schedules were well managed and we could keep an eye on each other. Here in LA, we were all dispersed to our own homes, so it was easier to get distracted or maybe oversleep or something.

"Should one of us call Silas?" I asked.

"I can," Elliott said and dug his phone out of his pocket. Less than a minute later he shook his head and said, "No answer."

"What the fuck do we do if our drummer doesn't show?" I asked, looking at Jesse.

"Let's not worry yet. I'm sure he'll meet us at the arena," my friend replied.

"He better," I grumbled and took a bite of the roll that melted in my mouth. Fuck, my man was top level with his cooking—way better than me. I could make scrambled eggs, and that was about it.

As soon as we were done, we all headed out. I kept my phone close, waiting for updates from Olivia, but my mind was already shifting gears. Sound check was crucial, and the adrenaline of performing was beginning to course through me.

We arrived at The Fonda Theatre in West Hollywood separately, and then quickly got to work. Silas showed up just as we were about to start.

"Where the hell have you been?" I asked.

He slid his sunglasses into the neck of his T-shirt. "Got stuck in traffic."

"Where'd you come from? San Diego?" Elliott teased. Silas didn't live that far from WeHo, so there was no reason for him to miss the barbecue and be late for sound check.

"Nah," Silas replied. "I was out in Huntington Beach."

"Why?" I wondered.

He smirked, and it clicked. He was with a chick.

"Say no more." I shook my head and then we all took the stage. I suppose being with a chick was better than being high on coke.

As we sat in the green room, waiting for the show to start, my phone buzzed with a group message from Olivia:

> Jasper's fine. The sting wasn't that bad, and the doctors are taking good care of him

I breathed a sigh of relief as I looked over at Jesse. He nodded with a small smile and then I went to the makeshift bar and poured myself something stronger than the beer I never got to drink at Jesse's.

The crowd was amazing as we sang song after song. I got lost in the music, the stage feeling like home. I tried not to think about Jasper, but occasionally, I would look in the front row, wishing he was there, but I figured he was back at Jesse's and probably sleeping.

Once the concert was over, we headed backstage, where we were doing a meet and greet with VIP fans. I played my part, taking pictures and signing autographs. Savannah and I even kept up our dating ruse and people were loving it. But the entire time, I wanted to bail. I wanted to get Jasper and go back to my place and see for myself that he was okay.

So, I did.

Getting into my Mercedes G-Class, I typed out a text to Jasper before I left the parking lot:

> Awake?

A few seconds later, my phone buzzed with a reply:

> Yeah. How'd it go tonight?

> I'd like to tell you in person. I'm on my way

> What if Olivia sees your car?

> I'll park a few houses down

Are you sure about this?

> I want you in my bed tonight

I don't know if I'm feeling up for that

> *That* isn't what I mean. I want to just be with you and wrap my arms around you

All right. I'll be waiting down the street for you ☺

19

Jasper

The smell of bacon and coffee had my eyes blinking open. It took a second for me to get my bearings and remember I had spent the night with Malachi at his place. The last time I had actually slept in his arms the entire night was after my winter formal when he got a hotel room for us. Otherwise, we were always sneaking around and slipping out of rooms before anyone could catch us.

I was about to climb out of bed and go find my man when the door opened. Malachi entered with a plate piled high with eggs, bacon, and toast in one hand, and a mug in the other.

"Don't get up yet," he ordered.

I shuffled back against the headboard, staying where he wanted me.

He walked over to my side of the bed and handed me the plate. "The bacon is a little extra crispy, but I wanted to make you breakfast in bed."

A grin spread across my face. "Thanks. That's so sweet."

He arched a brow. "Sweet?"

"What? It is."

"You can't call me sweet." He huffed. "I've got a rep to protect."

I chuckled. "Sorry. This was super-badass-rock-star of you. Is that better?"

He leaned down and pressed a kiss to my lips. "Much."

When he pulled away, I grabbed a piece of bacon and took a bite. While I would have eaten it even if it was burnt, he'd actually done a decent job. "I think I like someone else cooking for me."

He grunted a laugh. "Don't get used to it. There are several overcooked eggs and burnt pieces of bread in the trash. I almost gave up and ordered delivery."

"Maybe we'll start those naked lessons soon then."

"I won't say no to that."

After I finished eating, we hopped into the shower, where we spent time doing all the things we'd skipped the night before. It was nice he invited me over without any expectations, but I wasn't about to leave his house without taking advantage of us being alone.

"I should probably head back to Jesse's before they realize I'm not there," I said as I got dressed.

"Yeah. Do you know what you're going to say if he asks where you were all night?"

I shrugged. "Olivia was in her room when I left, so I don't think she knows I took off. And I doubt Jesse's even awake yet."

When we were younger, Jesse rarely got up before noon when he didn't have anything going on, and from what I'd seen on the road, nothing much had changed.

"True. He's usually the last one out of the hotel on our travel days."

I walked to the door, hesitant to leave but knowing it was time for me to go. One day, we wouldn't need to hide, but I understood Malachi's reason for not wanting to tell everyone yet. He loved me, and I loved him, and knowing that meant I would wait as long as he needed me to.

Thankfully, Jesse and Olivia weren't up when I arrived home, and I headed to the guestroom to change and then went to the kitchen to prepare lunch for them. My brother had told me I didn't need to worry about cooking while we were in LA, but it was the least I could do for him since he was the reason I was even here and got the opportunity to reconnect with the man I thought I would never have again.

"Good morning," Olivia greeted in a sing-song voice as she traipsed into the kitchen, Jesse hot on her heels.

I glanced at the clock on the microwave. "It's hardly morning anymore."

"Hope we didn't keep you up last night." Jesse laughed as he started making coffee for him and his fiancée.

"Gross." I pretended to gag.

"How are you feeling this morning?" my brother asked.

"I'm fine. Just a little tired." It was true but not for the reason he was likely thinking.

"What are you making?" Olivia peeked over my shoulder as I threw some pine nuts into the food processor to make a pesto sauce.

"Thought pesto pasta with chicken would be good."

"I'm going to miss your cooking when you guys get back on the road." She gave me a side hug.

I looked at her and furrowed my brow in confusion. "You're not going to be with us?"

Jesse handed her a mug. "She's staying here to check out some wedding venues and start meeting with the vendors."

"Oh." I was a little bummed to hear that. Over the last few weeks, she and I had grown closer as she hung out with me and Garrett while the guys and Savannah were busy with everything they did. "It's going to be weird not having you around."

"Yeah, I asked my sister to come stay with me before she starts classes at Hawkins U; otherwise, it would be too quiet in this house without you all here."

Jesse wrapped his arms around her waist. "Don't worry, baby. I'll FaceTime you every night," he said before spinning her around and kissing her.

I shook my head and turned on the food processor to drown out the sound of them making out. With how into each other they were, I wondered if they would have even noticed if I hadn't come home.

Once they pulled apart, I continued moving around the kitchen, putting the final touches on their lunch. As I plated the pasta, I felt my phone vibrate in my pocket. Pulling it out, I saw Malachi's name on the display.

Making sure neither Jesse nor Olivia could see, I clicked on the message to open it:

> I hate not having you here. Do you think you can sneak away again tonight?

> I don't know. Maybe if I wait until J&O go to bed

> I have an idea. Give me a minute

I shoved the phone back into my pocket then slid the plates across the island where Jesse and Olivia were sitting.

"You're not going to eat?" Jesse asked.

"I had breakfast before you guys woke up." It wasn't a lie, but a part of me felt guilty because I wasn't being completely honest with my brother.

While I started cleaning the kitchen, my phone vibrated again with a text from Malachi.

> Tell Jesse that Savannah is setting you up with someone. She said she would cover for us if he asks

I chuckled to myself. I was going to have to make Savannah some epic vegan meals to pay her back.

"What's so funny?" Jesse asked.

"Uh … Savannah just texted. She wants to set me up on a date tonight with a guy she knows."

Olivia smiled brightly. "That's awesome. Are you going to go?"

I shrugged, trying to play it cool. "Sure. It might be fun."

While they dug into their lunch, I texted Malachi back:

> It's a date

MALACHI TEXTED ME TO LET ME KNOW HE WAS WAITING FOR ME DOWN the street like we had planned.

"My date is here, so I'm taking off. Don't wait up." I waggled my eyebrows, causing Olivia to giggle while Jesse frowned.

"Don't we get to meet this guy?" he asked.

"Let's see how tonight goes before you freak him out with the protective older brother bullshit." I laughed.

"Fine," he grumbled at the same time Olivia said, "Have fun."

Once I closed the door behind me, I hurried down the sidewalk in case my brother got any ideas to follow me outside. Spotting the Mercedes G-Class, I swung the door open and climbed inside.

"Let's go," I said as I buckled up.

Malachi grinned and pulled away from the curb. "You that excited to get this date started?"

"Of course, but also Jesse wanted to meet the guy I was going out with. Didn't want to risk him trying to get a look at who I was with."

Malachi sped up, and I laughed. A couple of miles later, he merged onto the 101.

"We're not going to your place?" I asked, not remembering getting on the freeway the night before.

He laced his fingers with mine. "I know we can't do the official date thing, but we could go to the beach and hang out."

"You don't think anyone will recognize you?"

"We should be okay a little south of here. Plus, I brought a hat and sunglasses." He pointed to the ones on his face.

"Should I call you Superman?" I teased. "Or better yet, Clark Kent."

"Nah. I like it when you scream my name." He smirked and my dick twitched.

An hour later, Malachi exited the freeway and followed the signs to the beach. "I thought we could watch the sunset and then have dinner at a Hawaiian restaurant that's supposed to be pretty good."

"Sounds great to me."

After finding a parking spot, we climbed out of the car, and Malachi grabbed a blanket from the backseat and put his hat on his head.

"Shit. Where did Malachi Danvers go?" I looked around playfully.

He laughed. "Whatever."

As we made our way down to the water, I wanted to reach out and hold his hand, but I knew we were already taking a risk by being out in public. It was best if we didn't do anything too obvious to show we were a couple.

It didn't take long for us to find a place away from the other groups of people. Even though it was the beginning of summer, it was a bit chilly with the wind blowing, so it wasn't as crowded as I thought it would be. We spread out the blanket and took a seat just as the sun started to descend.

"Wow, this is gorgeous."

"It is," Malachi agreed. "I think the beach might be my favorite part about living here."

"Do you miss Boston at all?"

He looked at me. "I miss my family, but this feels like home too."

Glancing around to make sure no one was watching us, I placed my hand over his and squeezed. "It seems like all of your dreams have come true."

"They have now."

My heart raced at the thought of what those words meant. "I wish I could kiss you," I breathed.

"I don't think anyone would notice," he said before capturing my lips.

Although it ended sooner than I would have liked, I couldn't think of a more romantic place to kiss him than the beach with the waves crashing and the sun setting in the distance.

We continued to watch the sun disappear below the horizon,

enjoying the moment together. Once it was dark, Malachi folded up the blanket, and we began walking back to his car.

"Do you think you would ever want to live here?" he asked, catching me off guard.

"I don't know. I haven't really thought about it."

"What are your plans after the tour is over?"

I shrugged. "I was going to go back home, but ..."

"But what?" We stopped next to his Mercedes.

"I don't want to leave you."

"I don't want that either," he said, taking a step toward me, cupping my cheek and pressing his lips to mine.

20

MALACHI

The warmth of Jasper's body pressed against mine as his head rested on my bare chest. I blinked, trying to cling to the remnants of sleep, but the persistent ringing of my phone yanked me into full consciousness. I groaned as I reached for it on the nightstand, trying not to disturb Jasper but failing.

"Mm, what time is it?" he mumbled, still half-asleep.

I checked the screen. It was Rina. I sighed, knowing the call was unlikely to be a good one since it was unexpected. "Too early for this," I muttered before answering the call. "Hey, Rina."

"Malachi! What the hell is going on?" her voice pierced through the phone. "Have you seen *Star Nation's* latest post?"

"No, what happened?" I yawned.

"They posted a picture of you and Jasper kissing!" she shrieked. "And now there's a huge scandal because everyone thinks you're cheating on Savannah. The internet is going nuts! Malachi—" She hesitated, her tone softening slightly. "Is this how you planned to come out?"

My heart pounded in my chest as I sat up and stared down at Jasper. "No. No, it's not. No one knows I'm bi," I whispered, panic rising in my throat. "I'm not ready for this."

"Ready or not, the cat's out of the bag," Rina stated. "We have to deal with this now. The fans are losing it, and the press is hounding me for a statement."

Jasper's phone started ringing. He quickly grabbed it and showed me the screen with Jesse's name at the top. I shook my head to indicate not to answer it. He silenced it instead.

"I'm sorry, Rina," I said, running my hand through my hair. "What do you need me to do?"

"For starters, get ahead of this. We need a statement from you and Savannah. And keep Jasper out of sight until this dies down. The last thing we need is to add more fuel to the fire."

I nodded, even though she couldn't see me. "Got it. I'll call Savannah right now."

"Make sure you do. And Malachi," she paused. "Come to my office right away. I'll call Robert and get him to come with Savannah too."

"Okay." Robert was Savannah's manager. I figured working together to put out our statements wasn't a bad idea. "I'll be there soon."

The call ended, leaving me staring at my phone. My head was spinning, and I wasn't sure what to do. Was I happy I didn't have to pretend to date Savannah anymore? Was I relieved I didn't have to hide my feelings for Jasper anymore? He sat up and I felt his hand on my cheek, guiding my gaze back to him.

"What happened?" he asked softly.

"*Star Nation* posted a picture of us kissing," I stated. "Now there's a cheating scandal because everyone thinks I'm with Savannah. Plus, everyone is assuming I'm gay. Rina asked if this was how I planned to come out."

Jasper's eyes widened. "Oh, no."

"Yeah," I sighed. "I need to call Savannah and figure out how we're going to spin this."

Jasper's phone buzzed again, Jesse's name and picture popping up. "And Jesse?"

I bit my lip, worry gnawing at me. "This was not how I wanted everything to go down."

He silenced his phone again. "Me either. What do you want to do?"

"I don't know," I admitted. "But Jesse has always been protective of you, and I don't know how he's going to react."

"We'll face him together," Jasper said firmly, taking my hand. "We've hidden long enough. We deserve to be happy. Jesse loves us and sees you like a brother. He'll understand eventually."

"You're not worried he'll be mad at you?" I asked.

He lifted a shoulder. "I'm not sure I care anymore. I'm not a kid."

"I know, but he's my best friend and your brother. There's some unspoken rule about that."

"Does it matter since we're in love?"

I thought for a moment, then squeezed his hand. "You're right. We'll talk to him. But first, I need to call Savannah and handle this media storm."

Jasper nodded. "I'm with you, no matter what."

"I hope so because the celebrity news sites are going nuts."

"We should probably determine which side is my best side," he teased.

I laughed at his attempt to lighten my mood and leaned in, pressing a soft kiss to his lips. "I love you."

"I love you too."

While having a picture published of me kissing a guy wasn't how I wanted to come out as bisexual, it was the least of my worries since I wasn't sure how Jesse—my lifelong friend and bandmate—was going to react to me dating his brother. Also, maybe I didn't care that the whole world knew I was with Jasper because it was him. He was my heart.

When I called Savannah, she said she was getting ready to head to Rina's office with her manager. We decided to just talk there because we didn't know what to do. Rina and the label could figure it out and we'd do what they wanted. Except, of course, if they wanted us to keep fake dating.

Savannah and I were done pretending. She wanted to pursue things with Elliott, and I wanted to be with Jasper. It almost felt refreshing that everything was out in the open, except I hadn't spoken to Jesse yet.

I knew he was going to be pissed, but I hoped he'd understand why we'd never told him. From day one of Surrender, back when we were in middle school, I was known as the flirt of the band. It helped us gain exposure, and I never wanted to let the band down. Plus, I never knew how to tell Jesse that I was bisexual, let alone that I was with Jasper. But we were older now, and Jasper and I weren't only fooling around. We were in love, and that had to count as something in Jesse's eyes, right?

Jasper and I had a plan. I would drive Jasper to Jesse's so they could discuss the matter. Meanwhile, I would head to Rina's office and agree to do whatever Savannah and our managers thought was the best way to handle the matter. After I was done meeting with Rina, I would head back to Jesse's so I could work things out with my best friend. Except, when I arrived at Rina's, it didn't go that way.

I walked into the conference room and saw Jesse, Elliott, and Silas sitting around the table. Before I could ask why they were called in, Jesse sprang from his seat, his face twisted with rage.

"You didn't think to tell me you were messing around with my brother?" he shouted, charging toward me.

I had no time to react before his fist collided with my jaw, sending me stumbling backward as pain radiating across my cheek. The room erupted into chaos as Elliott and Silas shot up from their seats to intervene and Rina shrieked.

"Jesse, stop!" Elliott yelled, grabbing him by the shoulders and trying to pull him back.

I recovered my balance, but my anger flared. I lunged forward, grabbing Jesse by the collar and pinning him against the wall. "You think this has been easy for me?" I shouted, my voice shaking. "You think I wanted to lie to my best friend? You have no idea what it's been like!"

Jesse struggled against my hold, his eyes wild with anger. "Then why didn't you tell me? Why did you do it behind my back?"

Before I could answer, Elliott stepped in again, forcefully prying us apart. "That's enough!"

I released Jesse, my chest heaving. He straightened his shirt, still glaring at me.

"We're supposed to be brothers," he said, his voice filled with hurt. "How could you do this?"

"We are brothers," I replied.

"Well, you did a hell of a job fucking that up." He shook his head. "I need to get out of here. I can't look at you right now."

Without another word, he turned and stormed out of the conference room. I stood there, stunned and hurt, my hands shaking from the confrontation and my heart pounding in my chest. Was he only upset about Jasper, or was it also because I didn't tell him—or anyone—that I was bi? I wasn't sure.

Rina cleared her throat, breaking the heavy silence. "We need to focus on the issue at hand. Savannah will be here soon. We need to release a statement within the hour."

"All right. Is it from me or the band?" I asked, still wondering why my bandmates were there. I didn't mind, since we'd been friends for so long. Even though I'd hidden my relationship with Jasper from them, I was okay with them knowing the truth now. Hell, everyone was about to find out anyway.

"Since it affects the band, I asked them to come in," Rina clarified. "We all need to be on the same page."

I was surprised Silas was there and he didn't look hungover or high or anything. As for Jesse ... "Well, I guess one of you can let Jesse know."

Elliott put a comforting hand on my shoulder. "No, man. You need to talk to Jesse. This isn't over."

Silas nodded in agreement. "He just needs time to process everything. We all do."

I rubbed my cheek where Jesse had clocked me. "Yeah, I'll talk to him. You two are cool with me being bi?"

Elliott tilted his head. "Why would that matter to us?"

"Because of the band. We may lose fans now if they don't like the idea of me being with a guy," I replied.

"Fuck them," Elliott spat. "We're here to play music, not to get strangers' approval for who we date. If they can't handle you being yourself, then they're not real fans."

Silas nodded. "Exactly. Fuck them."

Relief washed over me. "Thanks, guys."

At that moment, Savannah walked in with Robert. She looked around, taking in the tense atmosphere and the absence of Jesse.

"Hey," she said softly. "What'd I miss?"

Rina waved a hand dismissively. "You know, just band drama. But come in. I was thinking the best way to handle this situation is to release a statement saying you and Malachi broke up recently, but didn't want to cause a rift in the tour. It's the cleanest way to manage the fallout."

Robert spoke as we all took our seats around the table. "I think that's a solid plan."

Savannah and I exchanged glances, both of us nodding in agreement.

"That works for me," she said. "We've been wanting to end the fake relationship, anyway."

"Good," Rina breathed, visibly relieved, and opened the laptop in front of her. "I'll start drafting the statement."

"Actually," Savannah interjected, glancing at Elliott before looking back at Rina. "There's something else we need to tell you."

"Oh?" Rina looked up from her computer screen.

Savannah locked eyes with Elliott as they sat side by side. "Elliott and I are together."

Rina's eyes widened in surprise, but it was Silas who reacted the most. "Wait, what? Since when?"

Elliott chuckled and grabbed Savannah's hand as she said, "For a little while now. We wanted to keep it quiet until after the tour, given Malachi and I were supposedly dating."

I nodded, a small smile tugging at my lips. "Yeah, and I knew, and I'm totally fine with it. We all deserve to be happy."

Silas blinked, processing the information. "Well, damn, seems everyone has a secret. But, hey, if you're happy, then I'm happy for you."

Rina sighed, shaking her head slightly but smiling. "All right, as long as everyone's on the same page. Let's get this statement done." She looked at me. "And you need to smooth things over with Jesse before tonight's show."

I wasn't sure it would be that easy.

21

Jasper

As I watched Malachi's SUV disappear, I couldn't help but feel conflicted. The night before had been perfect, but now the memory of us on the beach felt tainted because our private moment had been shared without our consent. My mind was a jumbled mess as anger burned deep within me as I thought about the paparazzi who believed they had the right to invade someone's privacy simply because they were famous. At the same time, my heart broke for the man I loved who felt he couldn't fully embrace his true self without fear of it negatively affecting his friendships and career. The only thing I knew for certain was he wouldn't have to face any of it alone. No matter what, I was going to stand by his side, even if it meant going head-to-head with everyone else, including my brother.

Slowly, I made my way up the walkway to Jesse's house. I had no idea what I was about to face once I walked through his door. At some point on the way over, he had stopped blowing up my phone, and I wasn't sure if that was a good sign or not. I really hoped he had been calling to check on us and wasn't mad, but if he was truly concerned, wouldn't he have texted after I hadn't answered?

As I stepped inside, it was completely silent. "Hey." I called out.

"Jasper?" Olivia responded. It sounded like she was in the kitchen, so I headed in her direction and found her sitting at the island, hunched over her phone. She looked at me with a sad smile when I entered the room. "Crazy morning, huh?"

I nodded. "You could say that. Where's Jesse?"

"I'm not sure. He stormed out of here after you didn't answer your phone a few times. I assumed he was going to Mal's place."

I supposed that was my answer about whether my brother was pissed or concerned. "Rina called him in for a meeting, so Jesse won't find him there."

"So, you and Malachi? What's the story there?" She sounded genuinely curious rather than judgmental.

"We're together."

"Wow," she breathed. "I had no idea he was into guys."

I shrugged because there was no point in denying it now. "So, how mad is my brother?"

"Pretty mad."

I went to the fridge and grabbed a bottle of water. "I don't know why, though. It's not like I'm dating some horrible guy. This is his best friend."

"That's exactly why."

Twisting the cap off the bottle, I took a sip and said, "What do you mean?"

"His brother and his best friend, the two guys who mean the world to him, kept a huge secret from him."

Damn, she had a point. I'd been worried about Jesse's overprotective streak, and never really considered he would be hurt by us sneaking around. "Hopefully, he'll come home soon so I can try to smooth this over."

WHILE WAITING FOR JESSE TO RETURN, I DECIDED TO CALL MY PARENTS since it was likely they would see articles about Malachi and me online. While they had been surprised he and I were dating, my parents loved Malachi and were excited for us. I never once thought they would have an issue with us being together, and it felt good to tell them finally.

After I got off the phone, I was tempted to text Malachi and see how things were going at Rina's because I was curious what was going to happen. Would he and Savannah "break up"? Would he make a statement about dating me, his bandmate's brother? Would he deny it was him? He was wearing a hat after all.

Before I sent him a message, I heard the garage door opening, and my palms began to sweat.

"Baby, do we have a first aid kit?" Jesse asked, putting me on high alert.

Olivia jumped up from her seat where she had been waiting with me in the living room. "Oh my god. Why? What happened?"

I was already on my feet when my brother replied, "I punched that fucker. And then I hit the wall on my way out and split my knuckles."

"You did what?" I roared, getting right in his face.

His eyes widened in surprise, but quickly transformed into an icy stare. "Get the fuck out of my face, Jasper. I'm pissed at you too," he growled.

"I didn't do anything wrong!" I shouted back.

His chest bumped against mine, making me take a step back. "You don't think sneaking around behind my back was wrong?"

"Give me your hand." Olivia pushed between us and started dabbing at his cuts with a wet paper towel. "Jasper, go sit down over there," she commanded, pointing toward the barstool on the other side of the island.

"He better be okay," I grumbled as I began pacing, too angry to sit down. "How did you even find him? He's meeting with Rina."

"He's fine. I was at the office because Rina called us all in since Malachi's actions have consequences for the entire band."

I stopped in my tracks. "That's what I don't get. I know Malachi has an image that you all are determined to uphold, but you guys backed him into a corner. Why should it matter who he loves?"

"Loves?" Jesse scoffed, pulling away from Olivia.

"Yes, we're in love," I admitted. Maybe if my brother realized it wasn't just a fling, he would be more understanding.

"You expect me to believe that? You and my best friend, who has never shown any interest in guys before or been in a relationship with anybody, just magically fell in love while we were on tour?"

The weight of all the secrets Malachi and I had been keeping from Jesse were crashing down on me. I knew I had to tell my brother the whole story because it would only make everything worse if he found out later.

"It's more complicated than that."

"Enlighten me then," he demanded, throwing his hands up in exasperation.

Taking a deep breath, I told him the truth about how Malachi and I had been together back in Boston and ended things right before they moved to LA. As it all spilled out of me, I watched my brother's expression shift from shock to rage.

"So, you've been lying to me for five years?"

My heart sank as I saw the betrayal and hurt in his eyes. "We didn't mean to hurt you. We just—"

"Stop making excuses!" he snapped. "I can't believe you guys didn't trust me enough to be honest. Nice to know you two think so little of me."

"Jesse, I don't think …" I wrung my hands together, drawing his attention to them.

"Son of a bitch, I'm an idiot. You were doing it right in front of my face with your fucking matching tattoos. Did you guys have a good laugh about me being so oblivious?"

Before I could respond, he stomped up the stairs to his room and slammed the door behind him.

"Fuck," I muttered under my breath and tugged at my hair.

"Hey." Olivia rubbed her hand on my back soothingly. "Just give him some time. I'm sure you guys can work through this. You're brothers."

I hoped she was right. "Yeah."

"For what it's worth, I think it sounds like the perfect forbidden love story."

I chuckled at her statement. "But how is it going to end?"

"That's for you to figure out."

Laying on the bed in the guest room, I pulled out my phone and finally sent Malachi a message:

> I just talked to Jesse

He responded immediately:

> How'd that go?

> Not well

> I'm sorry. Are you okay?

> Not really. I told him everything going all the way back to Boston

> You did?

> Figured it was better to tell him now instead of him finding out later. But I ended up pissing him off even more. Please don't be mad

I hoped he wouldn't be mad at me, because I had done what I'd felt was right at the time.

> I'm not. You're probably right about him being more upset if you didn't say something now

I blew out a breath, thankful he and I were okay.

> Okay, good. How did your meeting go?

> I'm still at the office. Rina's sending out the statement. Should I still stop by after to talk to Jesse?

> I don't know how receptive he'll be right now. Maybe he'll have calmed down by sound check

> You know you don't have to be there. I don't want to cause you any more problems

We had agreed to talk to Jesse together, and I wasn't going to let Malachi shoulder the burden alone.

> We're in this together. I want to be with you

> OK. Thank you.

A COUPLE OF HOURS LATER, I HEARD JESSE'S BEDROOM DOOR OPEN. I hopped out of bed and caught up with him in the hallway.

"Are you leaving for sound check?" I asked.

He continued down the stairs, not answering me.

"I'm riding with you."

He spun around. "No, you're not."

"Yes, I am." He could be mad all he wanted, but I wanted to be there for Malachi and my brother even though he didn't want me around.

"I'm not ready to see you and Malachi together. It'll just piss me off more."

"Too bad. You guys need to figure your shit out. You still have to perform together tonight."

"Unlike Mal"—he pointed at himself—"I actually give a shit about the band and won't allow my actions to fuck up everything we've worked so hard for. But if you're worried about your boyfriend, I'm leaving in two minutes."

We drove to the theater in silence. I was grateful he let me tag along so I didn't have to order a ride, and I didn't want to risk saying anything that might set him off again. All I could do was hope he would realize that no matter how angry he was at us for what we had done, it wasn't worth losing a twenty-year-long friendship with his best friend.

22

MALACHI

I wasn't sure if Jesse was going to show up for sound check. To be honest, I wouldn't have been surprised if he didn't. I also thought he might take a swing at me again. I wouldn't blame him because I knew he didn't have a problem with my sexuality. Based on what he'd said at the office, his issue was that I had been messing around with his brother behind his back. Dating your best friend's sibling always had a forbidden aspect, and a part of me worried that if things between Jasper and me didn't last, it would cause tension between me and Jesse.

I hated to think about me and Jasper not working out, but it wasn't like I could see into the future. What would happen after the tour? He had said he would be going back to Boston, so had he not even thought about the possibility of moving to LA to be with me? Would he even want to move to LA? Would we have a long-distance relationship? What about the next tour? Would he be our chef again? The situation was mired in so many variables.

In order to keep my bisexuality a secret and prevent upsetting Jesse unnecessarily before Jasper and I were sure about our relationship, it had been easier to not tell my best friend what was going on between me and his little brother.

But now he knew and was pissed.

Before arriving at the venue, I called my parents to talk about the photo that was circulating. They took the news that I was bisexual very well and when they learned I was dating Jasper, they were elated. They didn't press for more details, knowing I had sound check to get to, but it felt good knowing they were happy for me.

I walked into the Spanish-style theater on Hollywood Boulevard and saw the stage crew setting up and adjusting the lights and sound equipment. Elliott, Silas, and Savannah were chatting near the side of the stage, laughing about something. I spotted Jesse standing with his back to me, hands shoved into his pockets. He was talking to the members of Midnight Thunder, but glanced over his shoulder when I entered. Our eyes met for a brief second before he turned back, clearly not wanting to talk to me.

As I moved toward Elliott and the others, Jasper walked toward me, and my heart smiled at the sight of him. He reached me in a few quick strides and pulled me into a brief but tight hug.

"Hey, you okay?" he whispered into my ear.

"Better now," I replied, giving him a small smile as we pulled apart.

"The car ride was awkward." He examined my face as though he was looking for the spot where Jesse had hit me. Last I'd checked, there was nothing there yet.

"I hate this," I admitted.

"He has to come around, right? You guys have to play together."

"I hope so, but we could probably manage if he doesn't."

Jasper shook his head. "I don't like that."

"Me either."

He blew out a breath. "So, what does the statement say?"

"That Savannah and I are no longer together but we didn't want to announce it until after the tour. That it was an amicable breakup and we have both moved on. Mine goes on to mention my sexuality and how it has no bearing on my performance with Surrender."

"I hate that anyone who isn't straight has to explain themselves," he huffed.

"Me too."

"Let's go!" Jesse called, motioning for everyone to take their place on stage.

"Come with me back to my place after sound check?" I asked Jasper.

"Okay." He smiled.

I winked at him and then made my way to the stage, feeling the weight of the awkward silence between me and Jesse. Savannah flashed me a supportive smile as she stood off stage and waited until she was needed. Silas just gave me a nod, and Elliott squeezed my shoulder as he passed.

Sound check began, and we tested the mics and instruments, and after Midnight Thunder ran through a few songs, we did as well. Despite the music filling the venue, I couldn't shake the uncomfortable feeling between me and Jesse. His silence was deafening, and it took all of my effort not to let it affect me.

Finally, we wrapped up, and I stepped off the stage. As Jesse hurried toward the door, he looked over his shoulder at Jasper and snapped, "You comin'?"

Jasper shook his head. "Going to Malachi's."

"Of course you are." Jesse glared at me.

"Jesse, wait!" I called out and tried to catch up to him, but he put up his hand.

"I don't want to talk to you."

"You might not want to, but you should," Elliott cut in. "We can't let this beef affect the show tonight."

"The show will be fine." Without another word, Jesse stormed out, the metal door banging against the wall as he left.

"You guys are stressing me out," Silas stated. "I'll catch you all in a few."

We had three hours until we needed to be back for the show. There was no telling what Silas was going to do, but for me, I just wanted to have quiet time with Jasper.

Elliott pointed a finger at me. "Don't make me lock the two of you in a room until you figure this shit out."

"It's not me," I argued, stepping up to stand beside Jasper. "I want to work it out."

"I know. I'll talk to him after the show tonight." Elliott walked over to Savannah.

"Good luck." I motioned for Jasper to follow me so we could leave. Once we were outside, the paparazzi started snapping photo after photo. I glanced at Jasper, his eyes wide. Reaching for his hand, we bolted for my Mercedes. Questions were thrown at us, left and right: asking who Jasper was, how long had we been dating, had we gotten together while I was with Savannah. I ignored each one. As soon as we were buckled in, I got the hell out of there.

"Jesus, they are ruthless, huh?" Jasper asked, looking over his shoulder at where they still snapped pictures of us driving away.

"You get used to it."

"Do you?"

"I mean, it sucks having them practically everywhere, but it comes with the fame. Are you sure you want to be a part of this?"

"Absolutely," he said without hesitation.

"Even if it costs you your brother?"

"I don't think it will. He's more upset we didn't tell him than he is that we're dating."

"I hope you're right."

MY EYES LOCKED ONTO JASPER'S AS HE STOOD IN THE FRONT ROW, looking up at the stage as I sang the duet with Savannah. I winked and then looked back at Savannah. We were usually eye fucking each other during this part of the show, but tonight, it was different. It was almost as though I could hear everyone in the audience whispering about the so-called scandal. Maybe they were.

Once the guys and I sang our encore, we exited the stage. Sweat was dripping from every inch of my body and I grabbed a bottle of water and drank the entire thing in one long gulp.

"All right, guys," Rina said. "Great show. We have the meet and greet starting in thirty. Go freshen up."

We headed to Surrender's green room. Jesse still was not talking to me, but I was done trying to get him to hear me out. When he was ready, he could come to me. I didn't need his approval, and it was clear we could still perform without uttering a word to each other.

Grabbing my bag, I changed out of the tank top and jeans I was wearing and into a fresh tank top and pair of jeans. Jesse and Elliott did the same, but Silas was nowhere to be seen.

"Where did Silas go?" I asked.

"Said he left his bag in the car," Elliott replied.

I nodded and went to the small makeshift bar and poured myself a vodka soda. The door opened and Olivia and Jasper walked in.

"Great show, you guys," Olivia stated.

"Thanks, baby." Jesse stood and kissed her lips.

I wanted to do the same with Jasper, but also didn't want to add more fuel to the fire. Instead, I asked him, "Want a drink?"

"Sure." He walked up next to me.

I poured him one, and then we sat on the couch. We still had about twenty minutes before we had to put on a smile and pretend we weren't exhausted and just wanted to go home and crash before we headed back out onto the road. We had a show in San Diego the next day and would leave in the morning to head down. I just wanted to go to my condo, shower, and crawl into my bed one last time with Jasper before we were back on a cramped bus and sleeping in hotels again.

As the minutes ticked by, Silas still hadn't shown up, and the meet and greet was about to start. Savannah, the one who took the longest to change, had even returned so she and Elliott could make out in the corner.

"Where the fuck is Silas?" I asked again.

We all shared a look, likely thinking the same thing.

"I'll go look for him," I said, setting my drink down. Jasper gave me a questioning look, and I mouthed, "I'll be right back."

I made my way through the backstage area and out to Silas's car first, but it was empty. I headed back inside, searching every room along the way. Finally, I reached the bathroom. I pushed the door open slowly and my heart stopped at the scene in front of me.

Silas was passed out on the grungy floor, a bag of white powder lying next to him. The sight of his pale face and the shallow rise and fall of his chest sent a jolt of panic through me, so I rushed to his side.

"Silas!" I shook him, but he didn't respond. "Help!" I shouted as my mind raced. I fumbled for my phone and dialed 911 as fast as I could with shaky hands.

"911. Where's your emergency?"

I told them where we were, and what I thought was happening, and then yelled again for help from my friends.

"Come on, Silas, wake up," I urged, shaking him again. His breathing was light, his pulse weak. My heart pounded in my chest, and time stretched into what felt like an eternity.

The bathroom door flew open, and Jesse burst in, followed closely by the others. Jesse's eyes widened, and he quickly knelt beside me, helping to prop Silas up.

"Shit!" Elliott gasped.

"I called 911. The ambulance is on its way," I stated.

"We need to keep him awake," Jesse said, slapping Silas's cheeks lightly. "Silas, stay with us, man. Come on."

Security came into the small room, saw what was happening and muttered, "Fuck," before running off.

"Come on, Silas," I pleaded.

A moment later, the security guy came back. "Move out of the way."

Jesse and I pulled away from our friend and watched as the security guy administered Narcan into Silas's nose.

The seconds ticked by, each one feeling like fucking forever. But then, Silas's body jerked suddenly, and he took a deep, ragged breath. Relief washed over me, but I knew we weren't out of the woods yet.

"Keep talking to him," the security guy ordered. "We need to keep him conscious until the ambulance arrives."

"Silas, stay with us," I begged, dropping to my knees again and gripping his hand tightly. "Just open your eyes, okay?"

Jesse knelt beside me. "Come on, buddy. You're stronger than this."

Silas's eyelids fluttered, and he groaned softly. His eyes opened, unfocused and glassy, but it was a start. I squeezed his hand, willing him to stay awake.

The distant wail of sirens grew louder, and soon the paramedics burst into the room, taking over. They checked his vitals, started an IV, and loaded him onto a stretcher.

I stood back, watching helplessly. Jasper stood next to me and grabbed my hand. I held on tight, thankful for him and also scared out of my fucking mind. The reality of the situation crashed over me in waves. We should have gotten Silas help a long-ass time ago. We shouldn't have turned a blind eye because we knew what he was doing.

We should have helped him.

23

JASPER

THE WAITING ROOM WAS FILLED WITH STIFLING TENSION AS WE ALL awaited word on Silas's condition. It seemed Jesse and Malachi had reached an unspoken truce for the time being, but it felt as though it wouldn't take much for things to pop off again since everyone was on edge.

Malachi and I had come straight to the hospital from the venue, and Jesse, Olivia, Elliott, Savannah, and Rina had shown up only a few moments later. It seemed word had already gotten out that Silas had been taken away by ambulance, as indicated by the horde of reporters waiting on the sidewalk near the emergency room.

"Can't security do anything about them?" Elliott hooked his thumb toward the window where we could see the paparazzi standing around.

Rina shrugged. "Unless they come onto the hospital property, there isn't much anyone can do."

"I'm going to see if I can find some coffee or a vending machine around here. Any of you want something?" Olivia asked.

"I'm good. Thanks," I replied as Malachi, Elliott, and Savannah shook their heads.

Jesse stood. "I'll go with you."

"While you do that, I'm going to see if I can get an update." Rina followed them out.

I reached over and squeezed Malachi's hand. "How are you holding up?"

He'd been quiet on the drive over and hadn't said a word since we'd sat down. I could only imagine how scared he had been when he'd found his friend unconscious.

He shook his head. "Not great. I should have paid more attention to what was going on. All the signs were there, but I didn't help him."

"Hey, you're not the only one," Elliott said, leaning forward and bracing his elbows on his knees as Savannah rubbed his back. "I think we all wanted to believe he had things under control."

"This isn't anyone's fault," I stated. "Instead of blaming yourselves, you should focus on helping him through whatever comes next."

Malachi nodded as Elliott said, "We should probably listen to your boyfriend."

The words were spoken without a hint of judgment, and I was grateful Elliott seemed to accept us being together so easily. At least it appeared we had one of the guys in our corner.

Jesse and Olivia returned, and with them, so did the silence. After arguing with Jesse earlier in the day, I understood some of his reasons for being upset with Malachi and me. However, he was going to have to get over his shit soon because they were all going to need to work together to help Silas.

I didn't know how much time passed before Rina joined us again. She took a seat next to Olivia and let out a sigh. "Silas is awake, and he gave the doctor permission to talk to me."

"How is he? Do they know how he overdosed so fast?" Eli asked.

"It sounds like his coke was laced with fentanyl. He's stable now, so they're going to release him in a couple of hours."

"That soon?" Malachi balked.

Rina shrugged. "I was surprised too, but the doctor assured me it was standard procedure."

"He can't go home by himself," Jesse said, worry etched all over his face.

"He agreed to let one of you stay with him tonight," Rina explained.

"I'll do it," Elliott offered immediately.

"Okay, great." Rina gave a small smile.

"Can we go back and see him?" Jesse looked hopeful.

"No." Rina shook her head. "They said they would only let a family member in, but the doctor made an exception when he heard me at the nurses' station. You guys should go home and get some rest. He seems receptive to getting some help, and I want us all to meet tomorrow to figure out where to go from here."

"What about San Diego?" Malachi asked. "We're going to need to cancel, right?"

Rina nodded. "Yeah, I'm going to take care of that right now. As far as the other shows, that's part of what we need to discuss tomorrow."

After confirming Elliott would call if anything changed, we begrudgingly got up to leave. The second we stepped outside, the paparazzi swarmed around us, and we were nearly blinded by flashes from the numerous cameras pointed in our direction. They started shouting questions about Silas, and our group hurried across the parking lot to our various vehicles, ignoring the reporters' demands for information.

Malachi unlocked his SUV, and I slid into the passenger seat. Once inside, he started the engine and reversed out of the parking space. "Those fucking vultures have no shame. Why can't they give us a moment of peace?"

I placed my hand on his thigh. "They're assholes looking for a story. The only thing we can do is ignore them."

He blew out a breath. "So, are you staying with me tonight, or am I dropping you off at Jesse's?"

"Do you want me to stay with you?"

He gave me a small smile. "I figured that was the plan when you hopped in the car with me, but I didn't want to assume."

I squeezed his leg. "I want to go home with you."

"Good. Do you want to hit up somewhere to get a bite? I don't know about you, but I'm starving, and I don't have much at my place."

Normally, I would have offered to make him some food, but after the night we had, I wasn't feeling up to it.

I shrugged. "I could eat."

We spotted a twenty-four-hour diner not far from the hospital, and Malachi turned into the parking lot. We were seated right away and placed our orders. Since it was two in the morning, there weren't many other customers, and the few who were eating didn't seem to recognize Malachi.

"When we're done, can we stop at Jesse's?" I asked, as I dug into the pancakes the server had brought over.

He took a sip of orange juice. "Why?"

"I didn't really think about anything other than coming to see you tonight, so I didn't grab any of my stuff when we headed to the theater."

"You don't need clothes to sleep in, and I'm sure I have something you can wear tomorrow."

I arched an eyebrow. "I don't have a toothbrush."

"We can stop at a drugstore."

I knew he was trying to avoid running into Jesse, but with any luck, he and Olivia would already be in bed, so I could sneak in and out quickly.

"It will only take a minute, and you can wait in the car."

"Fine," he huffed. "But you need to keep all that shit at my house when we get back to LA."

I ignored the implications of what he said. It wasn't the time to talk about what was going to happen after the tour. But that didn't stop the happiness I felt deep down that he was making plans for us in the future.

When we pulled up to Jesse's, Malachi put his Mercedes in park but didn't make an effort to get out.

"Give me five minutes, and I'll be right back." I leaned over and gave him a kiss before climbing out.

I could see lights on inside, and I sighed. So much for hoping they'd gone to bed already. It pained me to feel disappointed that I might see my brother, but we'd had enough drama in the last twenty-four hours to last a lifetime.

As soon as I opened the door, I came face to face with Olivia.

"Hey," she greeted. "I assumed you were staying with Malachi?"

"I am. I just needed to get a few things," I replied.

"Is he waiting in the car?"

I nodded. "Yeah. We thought it was best not to get Jesse worked up again."

Olivia sighed. "This is ridiculous. The two of them need to sort out their issues now, especially with everything going on with Silas."

I wasn't sure if talking right then was best.

"I don't know. Everyone's tired. Maybe we should wait until after we all get some sleep," I suggested.

She pinned me with a look. "Just go get him. The sooner they talk, the quicker we can all move on."

"Fine. I'll be right back." I headed back outside. Opening the car door, I peeked my head inside. "Olivia wants you and Jesse to talk."

"Right now?" Malachi asked.

"Yeah."

"I'm not sure—"

"We might as well do it now because you know when Olivia decides something needs to happen, she won't let it go."

"Fine." He got out of the car. "But if he swings at me again ..."

"He's not going to punch you."

"He better fucking not," he muttered as we entered the house.

Olivia and Jesse were sitting in the living room, and I pulled Malachi over to the couch opposite where they were sitting. My brother had a scowl on his face but didn't immediately start yelling, so I took that as a good sign.

"Malachi, thanks for coming in," Olivia said, taking control of the situation. "I think we can all agree everyone here has a lot of hurt feelings right now, but you guys have been friends for way too long to let things fester instead of just talking it out." When neither Jesse nor Malachi responded, she rolled her eyes and turned to my brother. "Why don't you start by telling Malachi why you're upset?"

Jesse huffed. "It pissed me off that you two were sneaking around behind my back and it sucked finding out because photos of you two kissing were posted online. Then when you"—he lifted his chin toward me—"told me how it also happened years ago, it made me see red. It's like I don't even know either of you as well as I thought I did."

"C'mon, Jesse, that's not true." Malachi sighed.

"Really? Then why didn't you tell me you were into guys?"

Malachi ran a hand through his hair. "I don't know, man. It probably sounds stupid now, but at the time, I thought being known as the flirt and player of the band was important to our success. I worried if anyone found out I was bisexual, I would somehow ruin things for us before they even got started."

"Okay, but you could have told all of us. We would have kept your secret if that's what you wanted us to do. You're our best friend and should have known we would have had your back, no matter what."

I could understand why my brother was bothered by Malachi not being open with him. They'd shared everything growing up, so Jesse probably didn't think there was anything he didn't know about his best friend.

"I'm really sorry. Looking back, I know I should have told you. Maybe I had my own hang-ups about it, and I assumed you all would be disappointed if who I was affected the band in any way."

Jesse nodded. "Okay, I guess I can understand your reason when we were younger, but we've made it now. Why the hell didn't you tell me about the two of you instead of sneaking around?"

"Do you remember that day in the locker room when that kid Dustin was giving Jasper a hard time?" Malachi asked.

I cringed, remembering how embarrassed I felt knowing Malachi had witnessed that humiliating moment.

Jesse shrugged. "I think so."

"You told him you needed to approve of anyone Jasper wanted to date," Malachi continued.

"Sounds like something I would say." Jesse let out a small chuckle.

"Well, I happened to have a small crush on Jasper back then."

"You did?" I asked, my eyes widening because I had no idea. "I didn't think you saw me like that until the camping trip a year later."

Malachi smiled at me. "That's when I finally told you, but it started long before the night we kissed."

Jesse's brow furrowed. "You kissed during our camping trip? Where the fuck was I?"

"Sleeping next to us." I winced.

"You sleep like the dead, dude," Malachi added.

"Whatever," Jesse grumbled. "But you still haven't answered my question. Why didn't you tell me you wanted to be with my brother?"

"You always gave me a hard time about moving from girl to girl. I didn't think you would approve of Jasper dating someone with a reputation like mine."

"Guess we'll never know because you didn't trust me." Jesse rolled his eyes.

Olivia cleared her throat. "I think we can appreciate why you didn't tell anyone before, but that doesn't mean Jesse wasn't hurt by the fact you didn't trust him enough to share that part of yourself. And Jesse, as much as you're upset with Malachi for not confiding in you, let's not forget how poorly you reacted when you found out."

Jesse shifted uncomfortably, his gaze dropping to the floor. Olivia continued. "You lashed out and couldn't control your anger to the point you punched your best friend. We all make mistakes, but you need to take some accountability if you want to move forward."

"Olivia's right," Malachi agreed. "I messed up, and I'm sorry about that. I should have trusted you more and been honest with you."

"And I'm sorry for hiding our relationship from you," I added. "We wanted to be the ones to tell you and never meant for you to find out the way you did."

"I'm sorry too," Jesse sighed. "Obviously, the way I handled everything only proved you had a reason to worry about my reaction."

"Thanks." I gave him a small smile. "I hope going forward you can accept that we're together and be happy for us."

"All I've ever wanted was for you to be happy. If being together does that for you, I'm all for it." Jesse stood and pulled me in for a hug.

"Really?" Malachi stood.

"Really." They did their bro hug thing. "But if you hurt my brother. I'll kick your ass."

"You can try."

We all laughed, and it felt good knowing we were all okay.

24

MALACHI

The next few days were a whirlwind. Silas agreed to go to rehab, and in the wee hours of the morning, the guys and I drove him to a place in Malibu so we could avoid the paparazzi. The facility was perched on a cliffside, overlooking the Pacific Ocean.

We arrived just as the sun rose, which cast a golden hue over the tranquil waves. The facility's Spanish-style architecture, with its terracotta roofs and lush, landscaped gardens, looked more like a vacation resort than a medical facility.

"Man, this place is beautiful," Silas said from the back seat as Jesse pulled to a stop in front of the two-story mansion. "It's hard to believe I'm here for rehab."

"Yeah, it is," I replied. "But it's also the best place for you to get better."

"Yeah, man. We've got your back. Just focus on getting well, okay?" Jesse said.

Silas nodded, taking a deep breath. "I know. Thanks, guys. For everything. And I'm sorry about the tour."

Elliott turned in the front passenger seat to face Silas. "You and your health are more important than any tour," he said.

We'd canceled the tour for the next thirty days and hoped we could at least do our Boston shows and the final one in New York City. I was okay with putting the tour on pause because, like Elliott said, Silas was more important. Plus, Jasper had agreed to stay with me in LA since he didn't have a job or anything to go to in Boston. His sous chef, Garrett, did return to Boston, though.

"Absolutely," I added. "We'll be here for you, no matter what. The fans will understand."

Silas smiled weakly. "I appreciate it, really. I'll see you guys on the other side."

We helped him with his bags and exchanged a few more words of encouragement. I had thoughts of spending the next thirty days in a similarly cozy location. It wouldn't be rehab, but I pictured me and Jasper in a place overlooking the water in Hawaii or something.

"Remember, we're just a phone call away." Elliott clapped Silas on the shoulder. "Don't hesitate to reach out if you need us."

"Will do."

We each gave him bro hugs and then watched as he was escorted inside by the staff. As we drove away, the silence in the car was heavy, as we were all probably letting the situation sink in.

Elliott broke the quietness. "You think he'll be okay?"

"I hope so." Jesse blew out a breath. "He's got a tough road ahead, but he's strong. He can do this."

I nodded. "And we'll be here if he needs us."

We knew it would be a long thirty days for him, but we were ready to support him every step of the way.

"Pack your bag," I said as I entered my condo.

"What? Why?" Jasper looked up from the TV show he was watching.

"The setting of that rehab place was beautiful, and it got me thinking some time away might be good."

I really wanted to get out of LA for a while.

"Oh." Jasper's shoulders slumped.

"No, no, babe. I mean us. Let's get out of LA." I pulled him off the sofa.

His eyes brightened. "Really?"

"Hell, yes. Where do you want to go? I'll book our flights and everything. Hell, maybe even a private jet if I need to."

He looked past me as though he was thinking. "How about Cabo? I've always wanted to see those beaches and the Arch."

"Cabo it is," I said, grabbing my phone to make the arrangements. "But first, we need to pack."

Jasper nodded, already heading to the bedroom to start gathering his things. "This is going to be amazing. Just you, me, and the Mexican coast."

I couldn't help but smile at his enthusiasm. "And no LA drama for a while. Just you and me in paradise."

The next hour was spent packing and making the last-minute arrangements. As I booked the private jet, I felt a rush of adrenaline. This was exactly what we needed—a break from everything, a chance to recharge and find some peace. Just him and me being out in the open as a couple.

Finally, we headed to the airport. As we boarded the plane, I looked at Jasper, who was practically glowing with excitement. Seeing the look on his face made me hard as a fucking rock.

Once we landed in Cabo, we got into the limo I'd booked to take us to the resort where we were staying. Upon arrival, we checked in and got the keys to our suite, then followed a staff member who took our bags.

"Please let us know if you need anything, Mr. Danvers," the staffer said.

"Will do." I handed him a generous tip and he left.

Jasper and I walked into our suite and were immediately struck by its breathtaking ocean view. The sound of waves crashing against the shore was soothing. It was the perfect escape from the city.

"Look at this place," Jasper said, looking around. "It's amazing."

"Yeah, it is," I replied, taking in the luxurious surroundings. "Ready to hit the beach?"

"Hell, yeah."

We changed into our swimwear and headed down to the pristine sands. The resort's private beach was a stretch of heaven, almost too good to be true. We spent the afternoon lounging under a cabana, sipping on tropical drinks, and enjoying the warm weather. But it didn't take long for our peace to be shattered. From behind the palm trees, a cluster of paparazzi emerged, their cameras clicking incessantly.

"Ugh, seriously?" Jasper groaned, slipping on his sunglasses. "Can't we get one day without them?"

"Guess not," I muttered, trying to shield my face. I thought for sure security would have made it so we wouldn't be bothered, but someone at the resort must have tipped off the paps. "Let's move further down the beach."

We gathered our things and walked away from the intruders, hoping for a bit of privacy. But the paparazzi were relentless, following us with their lenses, snapping shots of every move we made, and yelling demands.

We tried to put on a brave face, laughing and joking, but I could feel the tension building inside of me.

"Hey, let's go for a swim," Jasper suggested, tugging my hand. "They can't follow us there."

We waded into the water, the cool waves washing over us. For a moment, it felt like we'd escaped.

Jasper floated on his back, looking up at the sky, and smiled. "This is what I came for."

"Me too," I agreed, trying to ignore the figures on the shore.

But as we swam, I could see the paparazzi still clicking away, some of them even wading into the shallow water for a better shot with their telephoto lenses. It was infuriating.

"All right, that's enough," I said, frustration boiling over. "Let's head back to the room."

Jasper nodded.

On the shore, I grabbed his hand, and we hurried to our room. Once behind the door and away from prying eyes, I pulled him into a hug. "I'm sorry. I wanted this to be special for us."

"It still is," he assured me, resting his head on my shoulder. "We just have to make the most of it, despite them."

He was right. We couldn't let the paparazzi ruin our time together.

We took a *long* shower, ordered room service, and enjoyed dinner on our private balcony as the sun dipped below the horizon. The sky blazed with colors, a breathtaking end to the day.

However, before we even got to *dessert*, my phone was blowing up with notifications.

When I looked at the screen, I saw a headline from *Star Nation* that read:

"Surrender's Malachi Danvers Spotted Enjoying Cabo Getaway with Bandmate's Brother"

25

MALACHI

The rest of our vacation in Mexico was spent in much the same way as our first day. When we ventured out of our resort, we did our best to avoid the photographers, but they were skilled at hiding and using telephoto lenses, so they'd gotten plenty of pictures of us to spread around.

By the time we landed back in LA, neither of us was feeling very relaxed from our trip. As we walked through the sliding doors of the private terminal at LAX to meet our driver, the all too familiar sound of cameras snapping photos and questions being shouted out started up.

As we hurried into the black SUV, I heard someone ask, "Is your relationship the reason Jesse's leaving the band?"

Jesse leaving the band? What the fuck?

Over the years, I'd gotten good at ignoring the paparazzi and their thirst for the latest gossip, so I tried my best to show the question didn't catch me off guard. It did, though. Was Jesse leaving? I'd always feared I'd be the one to make the band fall apart because of the secrets of my sexuality. Had I?

"What the hell was that all about?" Jasper asked as the driver shut the door.

I lifted a shoulder. "No clue. I should call Jesse to find out what's going on."

After the articles came out that identified Jasper as Jesse's brother, we'd tried to ignore all the speculation, but maybe we'd missed something major if rumors the band was splitting up were flying around before I fucking knew anything about it.

I pulled out my phone and dialed Jesse as our driver pulled onto the 405.

"Hey," he greeted. "Still in Cabo?"

"Nah. We just left LAX, but what the hell is going on? Are you leaving Surrender?"

"Fuck no. Why would you believe some bullshit rumor?"

"I don't know." I blew out a breath. "Guess I'm still not sure we're really cool again."

"We're cool unless you break my brother's heart."

I looked over at Jasper and laced my fingers with his. I gave him a warm smile and then said into the phone, "That would never happen."

"Good. And again, I'm not leaving the band."

"Well, that rumor had to come from somewhere, right?"

"Who fucking knows. People just like to start shit. They see an opening and want to make money off someone else's life."

"True. We need to debunk it somehow."

"Rina can make a statement."

I shook my head slightly. "I don't know. Feels like words won't be enough."

"So, what are you thinking?"

"Well," I cracked a smile, still looking at my boyfriend. "We could go on a double date."

Jesse snorted a laugh in my ear while Jasper's eyes widened.

"A double date?" Jesse asked.

"Sure, why not?"

"I mean, I guess that's what people do, but you better not fucking suck face with my brother in front of me."

"I can't promise that." I winked at Jasper. "But you're one to talk since you always have your hands all over Olivia."

"No, I don't."

"You do kiss in front of us," I reminded him.

"Well, she's not your sister."

"All right. You have a point."

THE RINGING OF MY PHONE WOKE ME FROM A DEAD SLEEP. OPENING MY eyes, I realized I was passed out on my couch with Jasper in my arms as we watched—or tried to watch—a movie to relax after coming home.

Jasper rose from our spooning, grabbed my phone, and handed it to me.

I sat up and swiped the answer button, even though I didn't recognize the number. "Hello?"

"Hey, Mal. It's Silas."

"Hey, bro. How's it going?" I mouthed to Jasper that it was Silas and he nodded.

"It's going good, but I heard Jesse's leaving the band?"

I closed my eyes, leaning back into the couch. "No, man, Jesse's not going anywhere. I promise you that. It's just some moron spreading rumors."

"Damn. One of the patients here had her daughter visit. Huge fan of ours and was sad we were breaking up. I had to pay a nurse to let me use her phone to call you and not the monitored line they want us to use."

I chuckled slightly as I envisioned him doing just that. "A lot of rumors are flying around, but trust me, everything's under control. We've got a plan in motion. You don't need to stress about the band right now. Focus on you and getting better."

"Yeah, easier said than done," he muttered. "It's hard not to worry about it since I'm the reason we're not touring right now."

"Don't sweat it," I replied. "We need you back healthy, man. That's the most important thing."

There was a long pause, and I could almost hear Silas wrestling with his thoughts on the other end. "Malachi," he started, his voice breaking slightly, "I can't stop thinking about that night and thinking about if you hadn't found me."

My grip tightened on the phone. "Silas—"

"You probably saved my life."

I swallowed hard, forcing the memories back into the box I kept them in. "You scared the hell out of me, Silas. Finding you like that ... it's something I'll never forget. But you didn't die. You're still here, and you're fighting. That's what matters."

"I know," he whispered. "I'm trying. I really am."

"I know you are." My voice cracked despite my efforts to keep it steady. "And I'm proud of you. We all are. You've got so much more life to live, so much more music to make. Don't let this beat you."

Silas was silent for a moment, and when he spoke again, his voice was softer, more vulnerable. "Thank you, Malachi. For everything. I don't know what I'd do without you guys."

"You're not alone in this. We're a family. We take care of our own." Jasper reached out to rest a hand on my thigh. I continued speaking into the phone, "You just focus on getting better, okay? We'll handle the rest. Don't worry about the bullshit gossip. Surrender isn't breaking up."

"Okay," Silas replied, his voice steadier now. "I'll try."

"Good. And remember, we're all here for you. Anytime you need to talk, you call me, all right?"

"Yeah, but getting a phone wasn't that cheap."

I chuckled. "We can afford it."

"I know. Thanks again. I'll talk to you soon."

"Take care, buddy." I ended the call and let out a long breath, leaning forward to rest my elbows on my knees.

"How's he holding up?" Jasper asked softly.

"He's struggling," I admitted, running a hand through my hair. "But he's trying. That's all we can ask for right now."

He nodded and gave my thigh a comforting pat. "He'll make it through."

"I hope so."

Jesse's Audi Q7 glided to a stop in front of the valet stand at the entrance of the Beverly Hills restaurant we'd chosen for our double date. We'd ridden together to show no animosity remained among us. We'd picked a spot popular with celebrities, knowing the paps would be in full force.

Jesse shifted the car into park and turned to Jasper and me in the backseat. "Ready for this?"

"As ready as we'll ever be," I replied and gave Jasper's hand a squeeze.

We stepped out of the car, and the valet swiftly took Jesse's keys. As we made our way toward the entrance, the paparazzi wasted no time. Flashes burst around us, their bright lights temporarily blinding me.

"Jesse! Is it true you're leaving Surrender?" a voice shouted.

More flashes followed, and suddenly we were surrounded by a swarm of paps, their cameras clicking furiously.

"Jesse, over here!" another called out. "Are the rumors true? Why are you leaving Surrender?"

He kept moving, Olivia clutching his arm tightly, her eyes focused on the ground in front of her as Jesse led her toward the doors.

"Jasper! Malachi! How long have you two been secretly dating?" My heart pounded, but I kept my gaze forward, my hand in Jasper's as we walked behind Jesse and Olivia.

"Any truth to the rumors about Jesse?" another reporter pressed, shifting the focus back to Jesse. "Will Surrender replace him?"

I'd had enough and stopped abruptly, Jasper's hand slipping from mine. My blood boiled as I turned to face the crowd. "Jesse isn't leaving the band. And as for Jasper and me, our relationship isn't a secret. We just prefer to keep our private lives private."

The cameras continued to flash and we pushed our way through the throng to where Jesse and Olivia stood at the restaurant's door. Once inside, the maître d' led us to a table by the window, which gave us a clear view of the paparazzi still gathered outside. It was an intentional choice because we wanted them to see everything was okay between all of us, an idea I'd gotten from when Savannah and I had our fake date.

Jesse pulled out Olivia's chair for her and then took his seat. Jasper sat beside me, and the entire time, I saw the flickering of the flashes outside.

A waiter appeared almost immediately and took our drink orders. Once he left, we all exchanged relieved smiles.

"Well, that was intense," Olivia said with a slight chuckle.

"Yeah, it's been a long time since we were the ones getting hounded," Jesse added, reaching for Olivia's hand.

Jasper looked at me, his eyes warm. "You okay?"

I nodded, leaning in to kiss him lightly on the cheek.

"No sucking face!" Jesse chuckled.

I grinned. "I kissed his cheek. But just know we've done more than that with you in the room."

"What?" His eyes widened as he gasped.

"Oh, god," Jasper groaned and tried to cover his face with his hand.

I laughed but didn't elaborate about the night of Jasper's eighteenth birthday. While everything was cool between Jesse, Jasper, and me, some things he didn't need to know.

26

JASPER

I stood in Malachi's kitchen debating what to make for dinner when I heard the front door open. "I'm in the kitchen."

A second later, Malachi walked around the corner and greeted me with a kiss. "You makin' dinner?"

"Don't I make it every night?" I teased.

He smiled. "You do, and I appreciate it more than you know, but I don't want you to think you need to cook all the time."

One of the many things I loved about Malachi was how thoughtful he was of those he cared about. He'd been the same way when he was younger, and all of his fame hadn't changed him.

I gave him another kiss. "Don't worry. I do it because I love it, not because I feel obligated." Moving to the pantry, I pulled out a bag of rice, deciding to make honey garlic chicken. "So, did you get Silas to the airport okay? How is he doing?"

Silas finished his stint at the rehab facility and was heading back to Boston to spend some time with his parents before the band performed there in a week. He wanted Malachi, Jesse, and Elliott to drop him off, since he said he'd missed them while he was gone. I knew the guys felt the same way, and I thought it was good for them to have some time together before he left.

"He seemed to be doing well, which was great to see. He's got a sober companion who will travel with him, and I think that will help him as we get back on the road. For now, I think spending time with his family will be good for him."

I opened the fridge and grabbed the ingredients I needed. "Yeah. I'm happy for him and a little jealous he gets to spend some extra time in Boston."

"Are you missing home?" he asked with a concerned look on his face.

"It's not the area so much because I really like it here, but it would be nice to see my parents," I admitted.

Malachi nodded. "I get it. I haven't seen mine since the holidays."

After getting a cutting board, I turned back to face him. "Do you think we could go back a few days early?"

"I don't see why not. Maybe all of us could go. I think some family time would be good for everyone."

"And maybe it will be a little more relaxing than our trip to Mexico," I teased, although there was truth behind my words. We had been lying low for the past month since returning to LA. The constant attention we received whenever we went out was something I accepted because I wanted to be with Malachi, but I didn't think I would ever be fully comfortable in the spotlight. "I'm sure you're tired of being cooped up here."

He lifted my chin and turned my head so I was facing him. "I've loved every second of spending this time with you."

He sounded sincere, but I still frowned. "Sometimes, I feel as though I'm holding you back from living the fun and exciting life you led before just because I'm not a fan of the paparazzi."

"Hey, don't ever feel that way. My life is so much more exciting now that you're back in it. I wouldn't trade what we have for anything." He pressed his lips to mine.

His kiss immediately wiped away any concerns lingering in my mind. "Maybe we can go out on a date in Boston."

He grinned. "I'd like that."

A FEW DAYS LATER, WE WERE BACK IN MASSACHUSETTS. JESSE, Olivia, and Elliott joined us as well, and everyone was looking forward to some time in our hometown. After our flight landed, Elliott took off toward his parents' place, and the rest of us swung by the hotel we were staying at to drop off our bags. Even though both Malachi's and my parents had offered to let us stay with them, we enjoyed our privacy and figured a hotel was a better option for us.

"So, what's your guys' plan tonight?" Malachi asked Jesse and Olivia, who were sitting in the backseat of our rental car.

"We're going to say hi to Mom and Dad and then meet Liv's parents downtown for dinner," Jesse replied. "How about you?"

"I'm having dinner with my parents." Malachi glanced at me and smiled. "Then I'm taking your brother on a date."

"Where are you guys going?" Olivia asked.

"We're going to a club," I replied. "No one even gets there until late so I'll still get to spend the entire evening with Mom and Dad."

When Malachi and I had discussed what we wanted to do, I'd suggested going to Chrome. And since we were looking for a place where we wouldn't be bothered by the media, it was the perfect spot. The nightclub took the privacy of its customers seriously. Celebrities and sports stars often hung out there; hell, I'd even seen the president's son there on occasion.

"You guys still going to brunch with us tomorrow?" Jesse inquired.

Malachi nodded. "Your parents invited mine so it's going to be a family affair."

"Nice," my brother said.

We pulled up in front of my childhood home, and Jesse and Olivia climbed out. Before following them, I leaned over and kissed Malachi.

"I'll pick you up around ten," he said as I reached for the door handle.

"I'll be ready." I kissed him once more and got out.

The second we reached the porch, my mom threw the door open and wrapped all three of us in a hug, squeezing us tight. "I'm so happy you're finally here. We missed you so much."

"Audra, let the poor kids breathe." Dad chuckled.

When she finally let us go, I wrapped an arm around my father's shoulders as well. "It's good to see you both."

Mom ushered us into the living room. "Come sit down. I want to hear all about what you've been up to and how the wedding planning is going."

JESSE AND OLIVIA EVENTUALLY LEFT TO MEET HER PARENTS, AND I continued to chat with my mom and dad. They filled me in on how things were going with them and asked me a ton of questions about life in LA. Eventually, they decided to head off to bed, so I went to my childhood bedroom, where I had stored some of my things when I first left for LA. I also wanted to set aside a couple of cookbooks so I could grab them before we headed back on the road.

While looking through a box, I heard a noise at my bedroom window. Assuming it was just the wind, I ignored it and continued my search. I heard the sound again a second later, so I walked over and opened my blinds.

"What the heck are you doing?" I laughed, lifting the window open.

Malachi smirked and climbed inside. "I told you I was picking you up."

"Yeah, but I figured you'd come to the front door like a normal person."

"You didn't seem to mind me sneaking into your bedroom before."

Memories of those nights years ago washed over me. It used to make me sad when I remembered those times, but now that we were together and everyone knew about us, it only brought me happiness.

"You're right. I loved it then, but I love it even more now, knowing we no longer have to hide."

He pulled me into his arms, and our mouths collided. I could easily kiss my man for hours and never tire of it, but eventually, we had to break apart and catch our breath.

"If you don't stop now, we'll never leave."

I shrugged. "That doesn't sound like the worst idea."

He shook his head. "I've got plans for you later tonight, and I'm sure you don't want your parents to overhear us."

Fuck, he was right. "Fine, let's go. But I expect you to deliver when we get back to the hotel."

He cocked an eyebrow. "Have I ever not delivered on my promises?"

No, he hadn't, and I couldn't wait to see what he had in store.

WE MADE OUR WAY INTO THE CITY TOWARD CHROME. When we arrived, the bouncer recognized Malachi as we walked up and let us in without waiting in line. As we stepped inside the dimly lit club, "Padam Padam" by Kylie Minogue was playing, and I was eager to get on the dance floor. Malachi grabbed my hand so we wouldn't get separated in the crowd and led me to the bar.

We ordered our drinks, and while we waited for the bartender to make them, I heard someone say, "Jasper?"

I turned to the side and saw Ryan Ashford standing there. "Hey, man." I smiled. "How's it going?"

"Good." He looked at Malachi next to me and glanced down at our hands, which were linked together. "Looks like things are going well for you too."

I beamed. "They are. Ryan, this is Malachi. Malachi, this is Ryan. I used to work for his father," I explained.

"Nice to meet you," Ryan said as he shook Malachi's hand. "Looking forward to your concert in a few days."

"Awesome," Malachi replied. "I hope you have a great time."

"Here are your drinks," the bartender said, placing our glasses in front of us.

Malachi paid while I asked Ryan how his dad was doing.

"He's great. His boyfriend moved in with him a few months ago, and he seems pretty damn happy."

My eyes went wide. "Boyfriend?" I knew Sean's wife had passed away a few years prior to me working for him, and I wasn't aware he'd started dating again, let alone dating a man.

"Yep," he chuckled. "Surprised the hell out of me too, but Declan's a good guy. And he cooks, so my dad's still eating well."

I snorted a laugh. "Wow. Tell him I said hi."

"I will. I need to get back to my table." He pointed to a group of guys who were watching us. "It was great to see you, and nice meeting you, Malachi. Maybe I'll see you at the concert."

"Sounds good."

As he walked away, I made a mental note to get him backstage passes for the show. Of course, that meant I should probably tell Malachi that Ryan and I had a bit more history than I had let on, but that conversation could wait until later.

We downed our drinks, and then Malachi leaned in and asked, "You want to dance?"

I nodded. "Lead the way."

The music pulsed as we made our way to the middle of the dance floor where the lights swirled around us as we began moving together. His hands wrapped around my waist, and he pulled me in close to eliminate the space between us. Just like I did anytime we were together, It felt as though the rest of the world faded away until I could only focus on the two of us.

"I love you," I said, trailing kisses down his neck.

His hand moved lower until he was grabbing my ass. "I love you too."

Song after song, we grinded together, and I could feel the heat building between us. After a while, I was desperate to get him alone.

"I can't wait any longer," I said in his ear. "Take me back to the hotel."

He pulled back, his eyes dark with desire. "Let's go."

27

Jasper

A DAY BEFORE SURRENDER'S FIRST SHOW IN BOSTON, I WAS MANNING the grill in my parents' backyard. We had decided it would be nice to get everyone together for a barbecue so we could visit and relax. The guys definitely needed the time with Silas, and it had been years since our entire families had all been together. Even Savannah was there to meet everybody.

"Hey, Jasper." Norah, Malachi's sister, came to stand beside me.

She was a year younger than me, and because of how close our families were, we had spent a lot of time together when we were younger. But I hadn't seen her since the finale of *The Band Showdown*.

I wrapped my free arm around her shoulder. "Hey, how's it going?"

"Just enjoying the summer off from college."

"You graduate next year, right?" While I hadn't seen her in some time, Malachi occasionally filled me in on what she was up to.

Norah nodded. "Actually, I'll be graduating after the fall semester. While I'm going to miss Hawkins University when I'm done, I'm looking forward to starting my career."

"Do you have a job lined up yet?"

"No, but I'm looking. Originally, I was searching for some marketing opportunities in New York, but last night Malachi and I talked and he offered to talk to Stellar Records to see if they had any internships available."

"Oh wow. I guess I'll be seeing you more often if you move to LA."

She smiled. "Does that mean you're staying out there after the tour?"

I took a sip of my beer. "Yeah. Obviously, that's where your brother is, but I also really like the West Coast. Plus, there are a ton of job opportunities out there."

"But it's mostly because of my brother," she teased.

"Pretty much." I grinned.

"I'm really happy you guys are together."

I started flipping the hamburger patties. "You are?"

"Yeah. Whenever I saw pictures of him out with random girls, I always wondered if they liked him for who he was as a person, or because he was Malachi Danvers, the lead singer of Surrender. You know the real him and somehow still love him." She chuckled.

"Geez. Thanks, sis, for that ringing endorsement." Malachi joined us, having caught the end of our conversation.

"Your fans might think you can do no wrong, but to me, you'll always be the annoying brother who picked on me when we were little." She hip-bumped him playfully.

He leaned down and kissed the top of her head. "Yeah, but you still love me."

She shrugged. "I guess." She may have enjoyed giving him shit, but the love she had for her brother was clear in her eyes when she looked up at him.

We continued talking until the burgers were finished cooking, and I took them over to the table, which was already filled with a ton of food. Malachi and I each made a plate and joined the group sitting with Silas. His parents were there, along with his sober companion, Cash, who came to meet the band since he would be traveling with us once the tour resumed.

"Hey, guys." Silas gave us a head nod as we took our seats. "Cash, you already met Malachi, and this is Jasper, his boyfriend and our chef on the road."

Getting introduced as Malachi's boyfriend in a casual setting still caught me off guard sometimes. We had spent so much time hiding before, but now we could be open with our friends and family without fear of anyone judging us. Finally, all those fantasies I'd had when I was younger were coming true.

"Nice to meet you," I replied.

"Likewise. This guy raves about your food, and if this burger is anything to go by, I'm likely to gain twenty pounds on the road."

"He makes some killer vegan dishes if you want something healthier," Savannah added.

I saw a hint of skepticism in Cash's eyes, but he smiled. "I may have to try one of those as well."

As the evening wore on, everyone seemed to be relaxed and having a good time. Off to the side, I watched Silas throw his head back and laugh at something Jesse said.

"Man, that's good to see," Malachi whispered, wrapping his arms around me from behind.

"He'll have challenges along the way, but with you guys in his corner, I think he's got this."

Although I had already known it, the day had only reinforced how deep the bond among them truly was, and I felt privileged to be a part of it.

Later that night, Malachi and I returned to our hotel room, where we cuddled in bed.

"Did you have a good time today?" I asked, running my fingers through his dark locks.

"Yeah. I didn't realize how much I missed everyone. It was nice having us all together again."

"It was fun catching up with your sister. I hadn't seen her in years, and she sounds excited to move to LA. I told her I'd definitely be seeing her around."

He looked up at me. "You're going to stay in LA?"

My brow wrinkled in confusion. "I told you I didn't want to leave you."

"You did, but I wasn't sure if you'd made a final decision."

I lifted a shoulder. "Well, I haven't talked to Jesse yet, but I'm sure he'll let me stay with him until I find my own place."

Malachi rose onto his knees and faced me. "You don't need your own place."

"I don't?"

He shook his head. "You should be in my bed every night. I can't think of anything better than waking up with you in my arms every single day."

"You're asking me to move in with you?" I grinned.

He smiled. "I thought that was sort of obvious."

"I don't want you to feel pressured, though. I plan to stay regardless of where I live."

"I'm not asking because I feel obligated and shit. I want you with me, so just say yes already." He leaned forward and planted a kiss on my lips.

"We're really going to do this?" I couldn't wipe the grin off of my face.

"Yep. We can move your stuff once the tour is over. In the meantime, I expect you to stay with me wherever we are."

"I don't know. You might get tired of me," I teased.

"Never."

I wrapped my arms around his neck. "Taking this job was the best decision I ever made."

"Agreed. Now let me show you one of the benefits of living with me. Get on your hands and knees."

I pushed my boxers down and rushed to do as he said.

"You have the most perfect ass," he admired, caressing one of my cheeks. "I can't get enough of you."

"Me either. Now fill me with your cock." I wiggled my butt, trying to entice him.

"Oh, I will, but I want to play first."

He spread my cheeks and circled his tongue around my rim. I lowered my forearms to the mattress and rested my head on them as I lost myself in how good it felt when he licked me there.

"I could eat your ass all night long," he growled and plunged his tongue into me.

"Fuck," I gasped. "I think I could come just from that."

"Not yet. I don't want you coming until my dick is buried deep inside you."

He continued to tongue-fuck my ass until I was certain I couldn't take anymore. "Malachi," I moaned. "I need you."

He grabbed the bottle of lube from the nightstand and squirted some directly onto my puckered entrance before using his fingers to stretch me. When I was ready, he replaced his digits with the tip of his shaft. Rubbing his hands up and down my back, he nudged inside me.

"You take me so well," he praised. "It feels like you're strangling my dick."

As he began to thrust, I moved my hands from the bed and braced them against the headboard and pushed back, forcing him to penetrate me deeper.

"Damn, you feel so good. Please fuck me harder."

"Your wish is my command." He picked up the pace and hammered into me, hitting the spot where I needed him most. "Is that what you want?"

"God, yes." I reached down and began jerking my cock. "Don't stop."

My arm started to shake, and I didn't know how much longer it would hold me up. Malachi's movements became erratic; knowing he was close had my balls tightening. Within seconds, I spilled all over the sheets beneath me.

"I'm going to come," he shouted as he gripped my hips so hard he'd likely leave marks behind.

"Do it," I groaned. "Come in my ass."

It didn't take long before he shuddered, and I felt the warm spurts of his cum filling me. He trailed kisses along my spine as my heart rate slowly returned to normal.

"If I weren't already sold on moving in with you, that would have sealed the deal."

He chuckled. "Such a smartass. Now let's go shower."

THE NIGHT OF THE CONCERT, I STOOD IN THE FRONT ROW BETWEEN MY parents and Malachi's. Silas's and Elliott's families, along with Norah and Olivia, took up the rest of the seats as we all watched Surrender perform.

When it came time for the band to play "Whispers in the Night" instead of standing together, Savannah moved over toward Elliott, and Malachi came forward to the edge of the stage. Not long ago, he had admitted he'd written the song about me and now was looking directly at me as he sang the words about his desire for what we finally had.

My heart swelled with love for the man in front of me, and I lost myself in his dark green eyes that reflected all the affection and desire in his lyrics. After he belted out the last line, he mouthed the words, "I love you," and crooked his finger for me to come forward. Once I was within arm's reach, he wrapped his hand around my neck and pulled me in for a kiss.

I expected a brief peck, so it took me by surprise when his tongue met mine, and he proceeded to devour my mouth. It was the most toe-curling, delicious kiss I'd ever experienced, and I was left breathless when he eventually pulled away.

The crowd erupted in cheers, likely having seen the moment play out on the screen behind the band, and I could feel the positive energy surrounding us vibrate through the entire venue. I knew if Malachi had any lingering doubts about how our relationship might affect the band, the acceptance we received from their fans would have immediately erased them.

AFTER THE SHOW, I WAS STILL BUZZING FROM MALACHI'S VERY PUBLIC display of affection. I headed backstage, where the guys would host a meet and greet. When I reached their dressing room, I slipped inside and went right to Malachi.

"You were amazing out there tonight," I said, kissing him.

"I don't know what the crowd liked more: our concert or the show you two put on." Silas chuckled.

"Yeah, everyone enjoyed my best friend making out with my brother." Jesse rolled his eyes. "But we don't have time for a repeat performance. Rina wants us ready in five minutes."

With a final press of my lips against his, I told Malachi, "I'll see you out there."

I made my way to the area, which was already filling up with fans eager to get autographs and take pictures with the guys. I had managed to get tickets for Ryan and his sister, Morgan, so I started to search for them.

"Hey, you guys made it," I greeted when I found them not too far from the dressing room.

"Jasper!" Morgan shrieked when she saw me and then hugged me. "Thank you so much for getting us backstage passes. I can't believe you're dating Malachi Danvers."

"Sometimes I can't believe it either," I joked.

They asked me what it was like traveling with the band while we waited for the guys to come out, and then Ryan's phone started ringing.

"Oh, man. I've been waiting for this call all day. I gotta take this somewhere quiet."

"I'll hold your spot in line," Morgan said.

"Don't worry. I'll make sure you get to meet everyone," I added.

Ryan nodded and took off down the hallway. A few seconds later, the guys came out of the dressing room and headed over to the table set up for them to sign whatever merch people wanted to get autographed. I followed them over but stopped in my tracks when I heard Malachi growl, "What the hell is he doing here?"

I turned in the same direction he was looking and saw Donnie Pierce, who we all went to high school with. He'd been in the same grade as my brother and his friends, but his reputation was well known around school for dealing drugs. And given that Silas had just ended a stint in rehab, I understood Malachi's reaction to seeing him backstage.

"You didn't invite him, did you?" Elliott asked Silas gently but filled with concern.

Silas shook his head. "I haven't talked to him in a while and definitely didn't expect to see him tonight."

"Do you want us to ask him to leave?" Jesse asked.

"Nah. There's no reason to cause a scene in front of the fans," Silas replied. "If he causes any problems later, we can get security involved."

After that, the meet and greet went on as scheduled, and by the time the last picture was taken and the final item signed, everyone was ready to head home.

"Tonight was great," Rina said as we all walked toward the parking lot. "I'd like to meet with you guys tomorrow to discuss the rest of the tour dates. I want you guys to start up again as soon as possible."

I knew they were all eager to make up for the canceled shows, but it was Silas who had the biggest smile on his face. When we reached our rental car, we said our goodbyes and climbed inside.

"So, are you ready to get back on the road with us again?" Malachi asked as he shut his door.

I grinned. "I'm ready for anything with you."

28

MALACHI

Four Months Later

As I stood with the Pacific Ocean behind me at Cypress Sea Cove in Malibu, the sea breeze blew against my face, doing nothing to cool me off under the late October sun. It was at least twenty degrees hotter than what I remembered Boston to be when I was growing up. While I missed Massachusetts, my heart was no longer there. *He* was standing next to me while we waited for Olivia to walk down the aisle.

After our show in Boston, we rescheduled the missed tour dates a few weeks later. Since then, Surrender had been back on track. Jasper continued as our chef on the road and once our final show was done in NYC, we went back to Boston, grabbed all of Jasper's stuff and he moved in with me in LA.

I leaned over and whispered into his ear, "I can't wait to get you out of that tux."

"Behave." He chuckled.

"I can't help it. You look so hot all dressed up."

"I feel the same way about you." He winked.

A sudden, loud whirring sound interrupted our flirting, and I glanced up in annoyance. A helicopter circled above, and I had no doubt it was paparazzi or someone working for a news outlet. The media was desperate to get pictures of Jesse's wedding, and their presence was always as bothersome as a swarm of buzzing flies. I shot a glare at the sky, wishing they'd just disappear. That they'd give our circle some peace at least this once.

"You've got to be kidding me," Jesse groaned beside me.

I clapped him on the shoulder. "Just drown them out, man. Just drown them out."

"Yeah, okay." He snorted.

"Don't forget you're the reason we made it big," I teased, reminding him he was the one to come up with the plan to try out for *The Band Showdown*.

"Where do you think we'd be if I hadn't suggested TBS?"

I glanced at Jasper and smiled. "Don't know, but hopefully we'd all be together one way or another."

A moment later, Midnight Thunder started to play the melody to a song we wrote for Olivia to walk down the aisle to. Jesse had asked the band—and our friends who had opened for us on tour—to play at his wedding. They were the perfect choice to help celebrate the day.

Taking a quick peek at Jesse, I could see his eyes were locked on Olivia as she held onto her father's arm and moved toward us. She looked radiant, her white gown flowing in the wind, her smile as bright as the setting sun. This was the moment Jesse had been dreaming about since we were in high school, and I couldn't have been happier for him.

AS WE MADE OUR WAY TO THE RECEPTION AREA—AFTER THE PAID photographer had taken a gazillion pictures—I walked over next to Silas while Jasper went to the open bar to get us a drink.

Not only was Silas not doing drugs anymore, but he was 100% sober, which meant no alcohol either. Having his sober companion with him all the time helped him a lot, and I had to hand it to him because he was doing amazing with his recovery. While we were finishing our tour, he was the first to wake up and do yoga while we all slept. He'd also had Jasper make him green smoothies every morning, and while I had never really noticed it before, there was now a little spark in his eyes that spoke volumes about his recovery.

"How are you holding up?" I asked my friend.

"Good. Just glad I could be here today to see them finally tie the knot." He smiled at Cash as he walked up and handed Silas a cup of water.

"I'm glad you're here too," I gave Cash a head nod in greeting, then said to Silas, "It wouldn't have been the same without you."

Elliott joined us, his eyes fixed on Savannah as she talked with Rina across the lawn. We were waiting for the bride and groom to enter so we could eat and really get the party started.

"How's it going with Savvy?" I asked, nodding toward Savannah.

He smiled wide, still not looking away from her. "Things are really good."

"Happy for you, man." I squeezed his shoulder.

"Thanks, bro."

Jasper walked over and handed me a beer. I kissed his cheek before taking a quick sip.

"Tomorrow—" Jasper started to say but before he could, the lead singer for Midnight Thunder, Adam, started to welcome Mr. and Mrs. Bennett. We clapped and then took our seats at the head table.

I was counting down the minutes because I had something up my sleeve for after Jesse and Olivia rode off into the night.

AFTER THE MEAL AND SOME DANCING, IT WAS TIME FOR THE SPEECHES. I stood up, holding my glass, and tapped it with a fork to get everyone's attention. "Ladies and gentlemen, friends and family, and those who are just here for the free food and open bar, good evening! For those who don't know me, I'm Malachi, the best man. And for those who do know me, well, I apologize in advance."

A little bit of laughter rose up from the audience, and I went on. "It's an absolute honor to stand here today as the best man for my best friend Jesse. But really, it's just as much of an honor to be standing here for Olivia too. You see, we've all been friends since high school, and I've had the pleasure of watching these two evolve from awkward teens who spent countless hours texting back and forth when they weren't together, to this incredible couple we see before us today who can't keep their hands off of each other.

"They truly are perfect for each other, so let's give a big thanks to Olivia's parents for raising such a wonderful person, and to Jesse's parents for raising ... well, Jesse. Seriously, well done on both counts!"

I glanced at Jasper and winked, wanting to thank his parents for making him too, but I continued with my speech.

"Now, let me take you back to our high school days. Back then, Jesse, Silas, Elliott, and I were inseparable. We tackled exams together, shared countless laughs, played our music in Jesse's garage, and got into our fair share of trouble. I remember the time Jesse thought it would be a great idea to sneak into the school after hours. Of course, he forgot about the security cameras. But that's Jesse for you—always full of bright ideas, like the time he wanted us to try out for a reality show."

"Yeah, and look where that got us!" he yelled and everyone laughed.

"Despite the occasional mishap, one thing was always clear: Jesse is a loyal friend with a heart of gold. Silas and Elliott can also vouch for that. And then came Olivia. Although she didn't join in on our high school shenanigans, it was clear from the moment she entered Jesse's life that she was someone special.

"Watching them grow together over the years has been nothing short of inspiring. From the moment they started dating, everyone realized they were meant to be. Olivia, you've always brought out the best in Jesse, and Jesse, you've always made Olivia laugh like no one else can. Your love story is like a classic high school romance movie, but with a much better soundtrack and way fewer awkward prom photos."

More laughter.

"May your life together be filled with joy, adventure, and all the happiness in the world. And may all your ups and downs be in the bedroom. To Olivia and Jesse, congratulations and cheers!"

Everyone raised their glasses, and we toasted to the couple. I took a seat and Jasper leaned over and said, "That was amazing."

"Thanks, babe." I kissed his lips quickly while Olivia's sister started her maid of honor speech.

As the night drew to a close, the newlyweds bid us farewell, stepping into a vintage car adorned with a "Just Married" sign. We all waved them off and then I turned to Jasper and said, "I have a surprise for you."

His eyes widened, but before he could ask more, a sleek black limo pulled up in front of us.

"What's this?" he asked, eyes twinkling with surprise.

"Just a little something." I opened the door, not waiting for the driver as planned, and waved goodbye to Silas, Elliot, and Savannah.

As we settled into the plush seats, the driver pulled away, and Jasper looked over at me. "So, where are we going?"

"You'll see soon enough," I replied, smiling mysteriously.

The limo navigated the winding roads of Malibu as Jasper looked out the window. I could almost hear his thoughts still wondering where we were going., I was tempted to tell him, but he would, in fact, know soon enough where our final destination would be.

"Are we heading to Santa Monica?" he guessed.

I shook my head, enjoying the suspense.

"Home?"

Home. I loved it when he talked like that, but we weren't going home.

"Patience," I teased, leaning in closer.

"I thought you couldn't wait to get me out of this tux?" he provoked.

I verified that the partition was up between us and the driver, then turned on the radio from the control above our heads. "We have some time."

"Oh, really?" He arched a brow.

"Do you think you can be quiet so the driver doesn't hear?"

Jasper's eyes flicked toward the front of the car and he lifted a shoulder. "Maybe."

My dick was straining against my zipper at the thought of him struggling not to be loud as I fucked him in the moving vehicle. "Guess we'll see."

"Oh, yeah?"

"Fuck, yeah." I winked and undid my belt.

He licked his bottom lip and got to work on his own pants. "Are you sure we have enough time?"

"At least an hour." I freed my cock. "Come suck me."

He slid off the seat and knelt in front of my parted legs. Without a word, he grabbed the base of my shaft and devoured me until I hit the back of his throat. Bobbing up and down, his tongue slid along the underside, coating my dick with saliva. With music playing in the background, I focused on the slurping of his lips as they sucked my crown before going back for more.

Even though we were no longer having to hide our relationship from anyone, the thought of being secretive in the back of the limo heightened the sensations, which were sending electric currents through my body with every lick and hum Jasper was doing, especially when he sucked my balls with his greedy mouth.

"You know," I said, watching myself go into his mouth. "We don't have lube." He looked up at me, his blue eyes sparkling in the limo's mood lighting, but didn't stop blowing me. "Guess we're just gonna have to use my cum."

He groaned and sucked me harder, as though the idea spurred him on. It didn't take long until I felt my balls tighten and I knew I was about to come.

"Babe," I said, and he pulled off and looked up at me. "Take off your pants so you can be ready for me."

Jasper nodded. While he sat on the limo's floor and got rid of his trousers, I lifted my hips and pushed my slacks and boxers down to my ankles. Once he was done, he returned to giving me head, and I slipped my fingers into his hair as I guided him up and down my shaft.

"That's it. Fuck, your mouth is so fucking perfect," I panted.

He hummed his response, and the vibration sent a zing straight to my balls. I tugged on his hair, and he pulled back as I wrapped my hand around my cock and started jerking off. He watched my fist slide up and down, but I wasn't watching what I was doing. Instead, I was looking at him, the man I wanted to spend forever with.

"I'm almost there," I groaned.

He licked his lips as if he was hungry for my cum, and while he usually swallowed all of it, we needed it to ease my entry into him and make him come as my dick pounded into his prostate.

"Hurry," he pleaded. Before he could reach out to help me, my hand stilled and I came with a groan, catching the creamy liquid in my palm.

Jasper got off his knees and straddled my hips without hesitation, then claimed my lips like he was starving to kiss me. We licked inside each other's mouths as I reached around and coated his puckered rim with my jizz and then slipped two fingers inside. He hissed as I worked them in and out, each time gathering more of my spunk to coat his dark tunnel.

He fucked my fingers and even though I had come minutes before, I was hardening again as our dicks rubbed together between us.

"Your fingers feel so good," he moaned against my lips. "But I need your cock inside of me."

"Are you greedy for more of my cum?" I smirked.

"Always."

"Then use me."

I slipped my fingers out and held the base of my shaft, guiding my crown to his tight hole. As Jasper sank slowly down and my cock stretched him, I reached above our heads and turned the music louder.

"That's it," I urged, as his ass swallowed more of me. I fisted his dick, giving it a few pumps to relax him more. "Take your time."

"I'm good," he breathed and sank all the way down.

"Now ride me."

And my man did just that, as the driver went around turns, over bumps, and got onto the 405. I jerked Jasper's shaft and swallowed his cries of pleasure as we kissed and he got closer to coming.

"I'm gonna come," he moaned.

I stilled his hips and leaned forward, laying him back on the sideways bench seat. Sliding out of him, I grabbed hold of his length and sucked him into my hot mouth.

"Oh, god," he breathed.

Taking my fingers, I slid them into his ass while I bobbed up and down on his cock. Within seconds, his body twitched, and he shot his load down my throat. I swallowed it all. Once he was sucked dry, I rose slightly and entered him again with my throbbing dick.

It didn't take long before I was groaning my release and shooting my hot cum into his perfect ass.

Laying on top of him, we caught our breath and then I grabbed a tissue and helped him clean up.

Once we had our pants on, we returned to the seat in the back of the limo and Jasper's eyes lit up with realization. "We're going to the airport?"

"Bingo!"

"And then where?"

"Do you want me to tell you now or do you want to wait until we check our bags?"

"Check our bags? You packed for us?"

I nodded. "Yeah. I had to in order to pull this surprise off."

"Now I'm really intrigued."

"You weren't before?" I cocked a brow.

"Okay, I was." He chuckled. "But, tell me now. Where are we going?"

I hesitated for a brief pause before responding, "Norway."

Jasper blinked. "Norway?"

"Yeah."

"What's in Norway?"

I cracked a grin. "You'll see."

THE CHILLY NORWEGIAN AIR GREETED US AS WE STEPPED OUT OF Tromsø Airport. It was nothing like California and for a split second, I wished we were back in LA. But that was only for a millisecond because I couldn't wait to see Jasper's face once he realized what I had planned.

The northern darkness was already settling in, with occasional glimpses of the moon illuminating patches of the landscape. A black car I had arranged waited for us just outside the terminal.

"Holy shit, we're in Norway," Jasper said as he slid into the car.

"I know. Just wait until you see our room."

The drive to Lyngen North was a journey that took us through an eerie wilderness, far from the city lights. Jasper pressed against the window, mesmerized by the mysterious scenery passing by. I stole glances at him, overwhelmed by how lucky I was to have him with me and how after all these years we were together.

Our arctic hotel stood as a secluded sanctuary overlooking a silent fjord. It was perched atop a hill and glowed softly under the moonlight. Stepping out of the car, the staff welcomed us and led us to our glass igloo.

"This is incredible," Jasper gushed.

"Yeah, the pictures online don't do it justice."

He looked up at the dark sky. "I can't believe there's a glass roof. It's kinda like camping under the stars."

"Exactly." I smiled.

"Ah, I see what you're doing." He nodded his head slowly.

I furrowed my brow. "You do?"

"I mean, I wouldn't have flown us to Norway just to go camping like we used to, but I have to admit this is pretty amazing."

As if on cue, the aurora borealis began to paint the night sky in green and blue light.

"Malachi," Jasper breathed, turning to face me. "Thank you for bringing me here. This is more than I ever dreamed of."

I took his hand, squeezing it gently. "There's something else," I began, feeling my heart race. Dropping to one knee, I pulled a small box from my pocket that I'd put in there when I'd changed out of my tux at LAX.

He gasped. "Mal …"

I swallowed and opened the lid of the box to reveal a black carbon fiber ring with a band of shredded green meteorite in the center. When I was searching for rings, the design had reminded me of the Northern Lights. "The day of our first kiss, you got stung by a bee."

"I remember." He chuckled slightly.

"I was so fucking scared, but I didn't want you to know. We played the questions game, and I asked you if you could visit any place in the entire world where would it be—"

"I said I've always wanted to see the Northern Lights," he answered as though he too was remembering.

"Right. You said it would be cool to see."

"It is." He looked up at the dancing lights through our glass roof.

"It is," I agreed and continued. "And I couldn't think of a better place than here to ask you if you'd marry me?"

"Yes." He nodded enthusiastically. "Of course, I will."

I slipped the ring onto his finger, the fit perfect as though it had always belonged there, and then got to my feet. Grabbing his face with both hands, I kissed him while the aurora borealis continued to light up the night sky with vibrant hues.

There were no paparazzi around to steal our moment. For once, we were just two people in love who no longer had to sneak around.

29

Ryan

Four Months Prior

When Jasper told my sister and me he'd gotten us backstage passes for Surrender's concert, little did I know meeting Donnie that night would throw me into the middle of a murder investigation.

Ryan's book will release on January 31, 2025. Add *Protecting the Witness* to your TBR and pre-order it now!

Silas and Cash are also getting a book on April 4, 2025. Add *Addicted to You* to your TBR and pre-order it now!

ACKNOWLEDGMENTS

We'd like to thank our husbands, Ben and Wayne, who help make sure everything is running smoothly when we are locked away writing. Laura Hull, Geissa Cecilia, Dan Jenkins, Stacy Nickelson, and Margaret Neal, thank you for the time you took to help us with this story. We are grateful to each of you.

To The Author Agency, Give Me Books Promotions, Jasmine PA, Tracy Ann, Nicole with Indie Sage PR, Wander Aguiar and his team, our street team, all the bloggers, and authors who participated in our cover reveal, review tour, and our release day blitz: thank you! We appreciate you helping us spread the word.

And to all of our readers: thank you for the support you continually show us. Because of you, we are able to pursue our writing dreams.

ALSO BY KIMBERLY KNIGHT AND RACHEL LYN ADAMS

Off the Field Duet – A MM Baseball Romance

Dibs - A MM Friends to Lovers Romance Standalone

Forbidden Series - A MM Forbidden Romance Series

Off the Bench Duet - A MM Hockey Romance

Butcher - A MMF Hockey Romance

ALSO BY KIMBERLY KNIGHT

Club 24 Series – Romantic Suspense

The Chase Duet - Spin off duet from Club 24 - Contemporary Romance

Halo Series – Contemporary Romance

Saddles & Racks Series – Romantic Suspense

Ex-Rated Gigolo – Spin off standalone for Saddles & Racks Series - Romantic Suspense

Sensation Series – Erotic Romance

Reburn – Spin off standalone for Sensation Series - Romantic Suspense

Amore – Spin off standalone for Sensation Series - Romantic Suspense

Dangerously Intertwined Series – Romantic Suspense

Burn Falls – Paranormal Romance Standalone

Lock – Mafia Style retelling of Rapunzel

Deliverance – Spin off standalone for Lock - Mafia Romance

Off the Field Duet – A MM Baseball Romance

Dibs - A MM Friends to Lovers Romance Standalone

Forbidden Series - A MM Forbidden Series

Off the Bench Duet - A MM Hockey Romance

Butcher - A MMF Hockey Romance (Coming Soon)

Audio Books

ALSO BY RACHEL LYN ADAMS

Desert Sinners MC Series
Mac

Colt

Off the Field Duet
Traded

Outed

Forbidden Series
After Hours Lectures

Secrets We Fight

Boss of Attraction

Taste of Surrender

Off the Bench Duet
Hooking the Captain

Retaking the Shot

Standalone
Dibs

Falling for the Unexpected

Butcher (Coming Soon)

ABOUT KIMBERLY KNIGHT

Kimberly Knight is a USA Today Bestselling author who lives in the Central Valley of California with her loving husband, who is a great *research* assistant, and young daughter, who keeps Kimberly on her toes. Kimberly writes in a variety of genres, including romantic suspense, contemporary romance, erotic romance, MM romance and paranormal romance. Her books will make you laugh, cry, swoon, and fall in love before she throws you curve balls you never see coming.

When Kimberly isn't writing, you can find her watching her favorite reality TV shows, including cooking competitions, binge-watching true crime documentaries, and going to San Francisco Giants games. She's also a two-time desmoid tumor/cancer fighter, which has made her stronger and an inspiration to her fans.

www.authorkimberlyknight.com

ABOUT RACHEL LYN ADAMS

Rachel Lyn Adams is a USA Today bestselling author who lives in the San Francisco Bay Area with her husband, five children, and a crazy number of fur babies. She writes contemporary and MC romance.

She loves to travel and spend time with her family. Whenever she has some free time, which is rare, you'll find her with a book in her hands or watching reruns of Friends.

www.rachellynadams.com

Made in the USA
Middletown, DE
11 February 2025